D0421827

The Girls on the 10th Floor

AND OTHER STORIES

Steve Allen

The Girls
on the 10th Floor

AND OTHER STORIES

HENRY HOLT AND COMPANY

NEW YORK

In Canada, George J. McLeod, Ltd.

Published April, 1958
Second Printing, May, 1958

Library of Congress Catalog Card Number: 58-7635

The author wishes to thank the magazines which originally published the following stories: "The Award," previously titled "A Prize for Mr. Big," Copyright © 1957 by Popular Publications, Inc. *(Argosy)*; "Joe Shulman Is Dead" first appeared September 19, 1957 issue of *Down Beat Magazine*; "The Girls on the 10th Floor," Copyright © 1956 by Esquire, Inc. *(Esquire)*; "The Secret" *(Collier's)*; "Blood of the Lamb" *(Manhunt)*.

80343–0318
Printed in the United States of America

To

William Christopher Allen

Contents

The Girls on the 10th Floor
AND OTHER STORIES

1

The Girls on the Tenth Floor

The Village is a pretty wild place. Something's always happening here, I mean. Like you take the place I stop in sometimes after I knock off work: Gus' Elbow Room. You probably know Gus. He tends his own bar. Yeah, the heavy-set fellow with the bags under his eyes. Fifteen years ago when I was a punk reporter for the *Trib* Gus was working as a doorman for Slats Ryan over on Eighth. Now he's got his own joint. Does all right too. Oh, nothing big like some of the uptown spots, but he's his own boss, you know what I mean?

You wouldn't think Gus would be a very rough customer to look at him. He isn't much more than five seven or eight and he looks fat. But that isn't fat. It's muscle. In the Village you never know when you're going to need muscle.

I remember one time I was sitting at the bar, it must have been about ten-thirty one night, and a couple of strangers walked in. Everybody in the village is a stranger in one way or another. In fact, a stranger bunch of people you will never meet in your life; but these particular strangers were even strange to the Village, if you know what I mean.

They looked like a couple of king-size trouble-makers. One of them was tall, raw-boned with big fists, and he rapped on the bar for a beer the way the fella tells you to do on television. The other was shorter, but he had a wild glint in his eye, like he was looking to pick a fight or something. They came in talking kind of loud and foul-mouthed and we all gave them the once-over when they sat down.

Gus is used to odd-balls, though, and they didn't faze him. Besides, the three guys at the far end of the bar were cops. Not that they could have been of much help to Gus, though, because they were all on the narcotics undercover squad, and when I call them plain-clothes men I want you to understand that they are wearing the plainest clothes in town: khaki pants and torn sweaters and longshoremen's jackets. The Village makes you as a cop in two minutes if you go in dressed in a business suit. You either got to dress in shantung pants and fancy shirts like a fairy or else you have to dress like a slob. So only Gus and I knew these fellows were on the force, and if any trouble came up it would have made a bit of a problem for them if they took part in the fracas inasmuch as it might have forced them to reveal their hand.

Anyway, the two newcomers sit down at the bar and right away they're shooting off their mouths and acting like a couple of cowboys in off the range or sailors back from overseas or something. Turns out they're just a couple of studs from Jersey City and there's no mystery as to what they're doing in town.

"Hey, Mac," one of them yelled at Gus, "come here."

Gus walked over politely.

"Where can we get some broads?" the shorter fellow said.

"I don't know," Gus said. Right away I knew he didn't like the boys. Actually Gus can tell you where and how to get anything in the Village. He's been around a long time and he has good friends on both sides of the law.

"Ah, come on," said the taller man. "You know what we're talkin' about?"

"Yes," said Gus, "I know what you're talkin' about."

"So?"

"So what?"

The tall man's face screwed up into an express of complete disgust.

"Look, Mac," he said, "we didn't come in here to make trouble, so why don't you be a nice fella? You didn't open for business yesterday. This ain't no goddamned tearoom you're runnin' here. I ask you again, where can my buddy and me get a couple of broads for the night?"

I got the idea Gus didn't like the way the fellow was leaning forward over the bar, making a face like he was going to spit.

"I don't know," Gus said. "Why don't you put an ad in the paper?" And he walked back to the other end of the bar.

I thought maybe there was going to be trouble right then and there, but something about the blankness on

Gus' face and the quiet way he said what he said must have puzzled the two jokers from Jersey. They just looked at each other for a minute, then hunched down on their stools and stared into their beer. Somebody dropped a dime in the juke box and Frank Sinatra began to sing. Gus and the three coppers started talking baseball.

Maybe it's unfortunate that this particular night Gus *wasn't* running a tearoom. Because after they got a few beers into them the two strangers came back to life. They sat muttering to each other for a few minutes, and then the big one jerked a thumb at Gus again.

"Hey, you," he said. "Come here."

Gus walked over to them.

"I'm askin' you for the last time, Fatso. Where can me and my buddy get fixed up tonight?"

"Where you fellas from?" Gus said.

"None of your goddamn business," the shorter man said. "You heard what my friend asked you. Why don't you answer him?"

" 'Cause he asked me too loud," Gus said. The coppers turned around on their stools, ready for action.

"Oh, a wise guy, eh?" the tall man said.

"No," said Gus. "Look, why don't you fellas just pick up your change and go home? It'll be simpler that way."

"Get him," said the short man, smiling with his mouth but not his eyes. "What are you, *tough* guy?"

"No," said Gus. "I'm a bartender. Not a pimp."

"What did you say?" the big guy demanded belligerently. I knew he was pretty drunk then. He was acting as if Gus had called *him* a pimp. The word was like a match dropped into a box of sawdust.

The big man got up off his stool and leaned over the bar. "What did you say?" he repeated.

"I said I'm a bartender, not a pimp."

"Over in Jersey we know how to take care of guys like you."

"This ain't Jersey," Gus said, not retreating an inch. "Why don't you get lost?"

The shorter man got up off his stool and in so doing knocked it down. The clatter of falling furniture charged the room with electricity. I got a grip on the neck of an empty beer bottle.

When the man had picked up the stool Gus suddenly said, "Wait a minute. I got an idea."

"What is it?" the tall man growled.

"You fellas are that hard up," said Gus, "I may be able to take care of you."

"Now you're talkin', Fatso," said the shorter man.

"Yea," said Gus. Then he turned to me. "Charlie," he said, "what's the address of that big hotel for girls over on Tenth Street?"

My eyes bugged out a little. There's no hotel for girls on Tenth Street, but there *is* a place called the Women's House of Detention. It's the city lock-up for young females.

"It's the corner of Tenth and Greenwich Avenue," I said.

"Thanks," Gus said, writing the address on a card. He handed it to the tall man.

"It's a big joint," he said, "but don't let that throw you. You're in the big city now."

The tall man threw a bill on the bar and began to move toward the door.

"Thanks, Buster," he said. "You wised up just in time."

"Incidentally," Gus said, "this place has great protection. They even got a cop guarding the front door, but don't mind him."

"Whadda you mean?" said the shorter man.

"He's on salary," said Gus. "He's just there to keep the peace. Don't take any back talk from him. If he gets smart just belt him one."

"You betcha," said the taller man. "We'll take care of him."

"Oh, and one more thing," Gus said. "The best dames are on the tenth floor. Don't let the madam give you any *old* stuff. Insist on the tenth floor. All young blondes, ya know what I mean?"

"Gotcha," said the shorter man and the two disappeared.

When the door was closed we all busted out laughing. Then I thought of something.

"Hey, Gus," I said, "that was a pretty good way to get rid of 'em for now, but what happens when they get wise?"

"Oh, I don't know," said Gus. "They come back and I bust their skulls with this." He held up a child's baseball bat that he kept behind the bar.

"All the same," said one of the policemen, "I wouldn't like to be you when they find out what's what."

"Well," said Gus. "We'll see."

I later found out from Stelmazek, the night guard at the Detention Home, what happened when the boys from Jersey got there. There's no sign out front, by the way, so Gus' trap was a neat one. The place *looks* like a hotel. When Stelmazek heard the night bell ring he walked over and opened the door.

The two men tried to walk past him. He shoved them back.

"Visiting hours in the afternoon," he said.

"We ain't visiting nobody, Pop," one of the men said. "Where are the broads?"

"What the hell are you talkin' about?" Stelmazek said.

"Here," said the tall man, reaching in his pocket, "here's a five-spot for yourself. Now lead us to the broads!"

"Get outta here," Stelmazek said and closed the door.

There was a moment of silence then several moments of vigorous pounding. Stelmazek opened the door.

"Look, Pop," one of the men said, "don't get smart. They warned us about you. Now don't get nasty again or I'll belt you one."

"Yeah," said the other man. "Stop the crap and let us in. And listen, don't try to give us any of the old stuff, you understand? We want the broads on the tenth floor. Cream of the crop!"

"Get outta here right now," Stelmazek said, "or I'll kick you down the stairs."

Another officer came along the hall toward the door, drawn by the commotion.

"You and what army?" cried the shorter man.

At that Stelmazek threw the door open wide and punched the shorter man in the mouth. He fell over backward and rolled down two or three steps. Stelmazek and the other officer leaped at the tall man and the three fell into the vestibule, fighting. The first man must have suddenly figured out the double-cross because he took to his feet and disappeared down the street, leaving his friend to do battle. To make a long story short I think the tall guy eventually did three days for disturbing the peace. I don't even know if they ever caught up with the other fellow.

That isn't the end of the tale, of course, because when we all heard what happened we figured it would be only a matter of time before the two guys came back to the Elbow Room to even the score with Gus. But weeks passed and nothing happened. We began to think the two had been smart enough to learn their lesson and stay on their own side of the river.

We found out we were wrong. One night about three months after their first visit the two men came back. I was sitting at the bar, as chance would have it, although I don't want you to get the idea that I spend all my time at Gus' place. I usually drop in two, maybe three nights a week, but for Gus' sake I was glad I was on hand this night.

That is, I was glad for a couple of seconds when the two Jersey boys walked in, but then I notice they're not alone. Behind them I see two other customers and they look even rougher than the first two. For a second I thought maybe they weren't all together, but I had guessed wrong. They all walked over to the bar very buddy-buddy and sat down at the far end, talking loud and acting for all the world like a bunch of guys who had come in to bust up the joint.

The three coppers weren't on hand this time either. There was only me and one woman at the bar, the cook in the kitchen, and two young fairies having dinner in one of the booths. It looked bad.

I know Gus had his baseball bat but we were outnumbered. He walked over to them as if they were all perfect strangers.

"What'll it be?" he said.

"Four beers," one of them said. "And make it snappy."

Gus didn't answer. He drew four beers and set them carefully on the bar. Then he walked down to the other end of the room and pretended to watch television.

After about five minutes I see the big guy jerk his thumb at Gus. I figured the time had come to do something, so I nonchalantly stepped over to the telephone booth by the men's room and put in a call to precinct police. Unfortunately it was Saturday night. It took half a minute for them to answer the phone and when they did they said they couldn't come right over.

"Look," I said, "nothing's happened yet but I'm pretty sure there's going to be trouble."

"We got a lot of trouble tonight," the cop on the line said. "But relax. I'll have somebody look in. May take twenty minutes or so."

I hung up. A lot can happen in twenty minutes. It takes two seconds to throw a glass through a bar mirror or give a bartender a clout on the head. I looked at Gus. He's dead game, that's for sure, but this time he looked worried. I looked at myself in the mirror. I looked worried too. Reflected in the mirror I could also see the baseball bat he kept under the bar. But I didn't know whether he'd try to use it against four men. There was too good a chance they'd take it away from him and use it themselves. Something like that is a good weapon only if you're fighting one or two men. Nothing short of a gun is any good against four and I knew Gus didn't keep a revolver on the premises.

Ten minutes ticked by. On television George Gobel was making everybody laugh, but he wasn't doing so good at the Elbow Room. It was pretty quiet, like waiting for a bomb to go off. The four strangers drank another round and their talk became rougher, louder.

Then it happened. The tall man of the original two stood up and walked down to our end of the bar. He leaned in toward Gus, who pretended not to notice.

"Hey, you," he said softly.

"Yeah?" said Gus.

"You're the wise guy pulled that smart trick on my friend and me a few weeks ago, ain't you?"

"Why," said Gus, "I guess maybe I am. Why?" He kept his eye on the stranger's hands, which were spread out on the bar, palms down.

"You think that was a very nice thing to do?" said the man.

"I don't know," said Gus. "It just came to me at the time. Maybe you guys were askin' for it. What's the matter, can't you take a joke?"

"Yeah, sure," the man said. "I can take a joke. Don't you worry about that. In fact, that's what I want to talk to you about. Come here," he gestured. "I wanna whisper something to you."

I turned partly sideways so that when he made his move I could get a good shot at him. I figured if we could get one of them out of the way fast we might stand a chance against the other three.

Gus leaned forward, warily. His right hand was out of sight behind the bar.

"What do you want?" he said.

"Well, I'll tell you," said the stranger. "At first me and my buddy were pretty sore, but you see them two guys we brought in with us? We want you to do us a favor."

"What?" said Gus, his jaw dropping.

"I'm gonna call you down to the other end of the bar in a minute and ask you about some broads for our two friends. I want you to hook them just the way you hooked us. Okay?"

"Okay," said Gus, bringing his right hand back up into sight.

Before the four guys left, Gus set up a round on the house. I had a shot myself.

2

If People Would Only Think

Fox had a limousine waiting for her at the airport. The driver got her baggage and they drove sedately, in a drizzling rain, to the Sherry-Netherland.

At the desk the manager said, "Good morning, Miss Arlen. Nice to have you with us again."

She smiled wearily, removed her dark glasses, and dropped them into her bag. As soon as she was admitted to her suite she walked to the phone and called Billie.

"Billie, darling," she said, "I just got off the plane and I'm dead. Can you come right over?"

"Not right away, Miss Arlen," Billie said. "I've got somebody at one o'clock, but I can come over after that."

"All right, dear. That will be fine. Don't be late. I'm a wreck."

She hung up the phone, took off her clothes, and soaked for twenty minutes in a hot tub. While she was drying herself, looking at her body in the mirror, the phone rang and in crossing the room to answer it she left dainty, moist footprints on the beige rug. It was a man from the Morris office. She told him she was too busy to talk to anybody, suggested he call back the following day, and after he had said, "If you need anything give us a call," she agreed that she would, sang a good-by, and then walked slowly to the window, holding the towel in front of her. The city looked good, even in the rain. Two or three times a year she passed through an I'm-going-to-sell-the-house-in-Bel-Air-and-move-to-New York mood, but the feeling never seemed to stick.

She had some lunch sent up.

Shortly after two Billie arrived.

"How've you been?" she said.

"Oh, you know," Monica Arlen answered. "A little of this and a little of that. I'll fix the bed."

She pulled back the spread and blankets and one sheet and then placed three bath towels on the bed to soak up any massage oils that might drip from her body. Billie walked into the bathroom, removed her street clothes, and changed to the familiar white Dacron nurse's dress.

Monica lay face down on the terry cloth and closed her eyes while Billie sat on the edge of the bed and worked on her feet.

"Have your sinuses been bothering you?" she asked.

Monica said they had not. "Well," she added, "maybe last week, a little."

"I thought so," Billie said. "Feels a little tight around the ball of the foot. That's the sinuses. You still have the headaches?"

"Now and then."

"I'll work on the big toe. Clear that right up."

"That feels good," Monica said.

"How's *Mister* Brinkley?" Billie said.

"Fine," Monica said. "He'll be coming in in about two weeks. Right now he's taking Tim back to Saint Mark's."

"What year is he in now?"

"Well, let's see," Monica said. "He's fourteen; that should mean he's in first or second year high, but he had the trouble the last two years, you know, and he's not quite up to where he should be."

"That's too bad," Billie said, sighing.

"I've been at my wits' end," Monica said. "I don't think there's anybody left in the world who knows how to do my hair. Abby used to do it beautifully, damn him, but he got so he just couldn't take criticism and you know how it is, darling, you get so tired of having to be *nice* to people. I finally told him what he could do with the whole rotten business so I've got to find somebody else."

"That's too bad," Billie said.

Monica belched and said, "Excuse me. I've got terrible gas."

"It's coffee, probably," Billie said.

"Yes," Monica said. "I had some on the plane."

"Sedgewick Carver says we poison ourselves at the breakfast table."

"Who says?"

"You remember," Billie said. "That book I gave you last time. *Starvation Amid Plenty*."

"Oh, yes," Monica said. "Marvelous. Absolutely marvelous. I must finish reading it. Good God, I must finish reading *something*. I've had three scripts on my desk out there

for the past month, and I tell you I haven't had a minute
to even look at them."

"You're working too hard," Billie said.

"I know it," Monica said. "They'll work you to death
out there if you let them."

"When is your next picture?"

"Well, there's nothing actually about to come out,"
Monica said. "I mean, nothing I'd want anybody to see.
There's a terrible mish-mosh I did at U-I, but it's practically science fiction or something. Anyway, it won't be out
till spring."

"What happened to the thing you were talking about
with Jimmy Stewart?"

"I turned them down on that one, my dear, and fast. I
mean Jimmy's a darling and all, but when you have a price
you have a price. Besides, the part wasn't the one I thought
they meant. When they first called me, I mean. Ah," she
sighed, "that feels good."

"Good," Billie said. "Right there?"

"Yes," Monica said.

"Will Mr. Brinkley be able to stay when he comes in?"

"No," Monica said. "Oh, he'll be here for a few days,
but then he has to go to a sales convention, or something,
in Chicago, I think it is."

"Is he bringing the girls?"

"No, they're spending the season with my first husband,"
Monica said. "I wanted to have them with us, but I wasn't
sure that it wouldn't be too much of a strain on Ralph. I
mean he's an angel and all, but after all, they are another
man's children."

"Yes," Billie said, massaging the left thigh.

"Susan acted like a devil the last time we were all together," Monica said. "We put her to bed in Ralph's room —he was out of town—and she got a scissors and cut about ten of his most beautiful ties to pieces. Thank God he never noticed it, but I could see that it wasn't going to work out, so I called Tom and told him how things stood. He has them at Palm Springs right now."

"That's nice," Billie said. "Have you lost weight?"

"Who knows?" Monica said. "I've been doing those damned stomach exercises you told me about, but I don't know how much good it's done me."

"Are you still taking the vitamins?"

"The ones you gave me?"

"Yes."

"Yes, I am. They're wonderful. I've also been taking the alfalfa pills and we're serving nothing, but nothing, but that royal Queenbee jelly or whatever you call it."

"That's good," Billie said. "Dr. Torrance says it's good for the nerves. You ought to come to one of his lectures sometimes."

"I'd love to, Billie," Monica said, "but I won't have a minute. Absolutely not one blessed minute."

"He says that honey is a natural sugar. That's the thing he preaches. Natural foods. And no aluminum cooking-ware."

"You don't say."

"Yes," Billie said. "It's just like he says. If people would only think, they'd realize."

"They certainly would," Monica said.

Billie worked silently for several minutes and then said, "You're pretty tight in through here. Pituitary."

"I *have* been feeling tense the last few days."

"Dr. Torrance says the pituitary is the key to health.

I'll work the blood loose here. When the nerves and muscles are tense it restricts the flow of blood."

"Naturally," Monica said.

"I saw a picture of you and all four of the kids in *Modern Screen*," Billie said.

"Oh, that luncheon thing?"

"Yes. I mean I forget what it was but you had a big hat and the kids were——"

"Yes," Monica said. "That was the luncheon at the Beverly Hills. Everybody and their kids were there."

"The kids looked so nice and neat and lovely with their white gloves and all."

"What did you think of the hat?"

"What hat?"

"The hat I was wearing."

"Oh, it was lovely. Were you all in white?"

"No, just the children. I had on a perfectly adorable aqua blue dress and a matching hat. Very light. It photographed white."

"The kids looked lovely. So neat and all."

"Yes, they did, the little darlings. I think they were the only children there that day with any manners. Honestly, it's gotten so people don't know how to raise children."

"Isn't it terrible?" Billie said.

"Unbelievable. That's one thing I've always insisted on from mine is obedience. Tom always gave me credit for that. He always said I made those kids toe the mark. I mean, after all, the time to start is while they're young. They'll never learn later."

"You're so right," Billie said, massaging the upper back.

"I mean if you don't teach them obedience and manners they can drive you crazy. Maybe a fishwife can have them around the house screaming from morning to night and it's all right, but when I get home from the studio after being on my feet all day I've got to have peace and quiet, and where are you going to get it, God knows, if not in your own home?"

"Right."

"Tom used to say I was being too strict, but I said to him, 'Nonsense,' I said. I said, 'My God, parents have rights as well as children and the day will come when they'll thank me for it,' I said."

"They looked so nice with their little white gloves."

"Of course," Monica said. "I believe in giving them the best. The best clothes. The best boarding schools. The best medical care. Jimmy still wets the bed, you know, and the doctor says it's not too unusual for an eleven-year-old . . . but I think if you give them the best of everything, plus discipline, in the long run it'll build real character for them."

"That's right," Billie said. "If people would only think."

3

My Little Darling

From the outside there appeared nothing unusual about the home of the Taylors. It was a large, two-story wooden structure that had had, when it was new, an air of elegance about it. Since the time of the first World War, however, it had fallen into gradual, graceful decay, as had all the other houses on Pine Street. The neighborhood was far from being a slum; it had not even degenerated to the point where the larger homes had been converted into rooming houses, as had happened in other parts of the city. But the entire area had a delicately tired air about it. The young families of the '20's were now old, the children fully grown and moved away, and Pine and the surrounding streets were quiet, partly because the vital heart of the city had slipped away almost unnoticed to another section of the town and partly because there were no children playing in the streets. It was a neighborhood of old houses, old trees, and old people.

Perhaps the youngest couple in the neighborhood were the Taylors. Mr. Taylor was just under fifty and his wife was five years older. They lived alone in the big house on the corner of Pine and Fourth, although they had not always lived alone. One child had been born to them but it had died in the influenza epidemic of 1918, at the age of four. It had been called Timothy. Timothy, Junior. Mrs. Taylor had decided on the name because her husband's name had always fascinated her in that it had a certain rhythm as it rolled off the tongue.

"Timothy Taylor," she would say, rolling her head. "Timothy Taylor, Timothy Tie. Timothy-Bimothy-Hy-dle-dee-eye." Mrs. Taylor liked poetry, if it had a good meter and a beat to it. She had some musical talent, cried easily, and was extremely maternal. The death of young Timothy had shocked her so deeply that she remained in mourning for almost half a year; and even after that her friends were given to understand by Mr. Taylor that they might not bring children to visit, that they might not mention influenza, and that they might not laugh raucously in the Taylor house.

Fortunately, Mrs. Taylor was devoted to her husband and upon him she lavished the motherly affection that she would have directed toward the child. Since Mr. Taylor was the sort of man who enjoyed being pampered, this worked out admirably. He hugely relished being served breakfast in bed, and two or three mornings a week was pleased to see Mrs. Taylor, who always got up first, glid-ing back into the room with a large tray laden with toast, coffee, orange juice, marmalade, and eggs.

He would always pretend to be surprised at such times.

"Now, now," he would say, "you shouldn't be doing this, Mildred. You shouldn't be doing this at all."

"Ne-ver mi-i-i-nd," Mrs. Taylor would coo. "I'm just bringing my little darling his breakfast in his little bed." Then she would put the tray down on the side table, prop Mr. Taylor up with two pillows behind him, give him a kiss, and put the tray carefully on his lap. He would sit, feeling slightly guilty but very pleased, munching his toast and sipping his coffee, and he and Mrs. Taylor would discuss their plans for the day. Not many people in the neighborhood understood exactly what it was that Mr. Taylor "did," but this was understandable for the reason that he didn't do much of anything, especially during the latter years. He just "had money," and although as a younger man he had worked for a time at his uncle's bank, and for a shorter period had been employed with a brokerage firm, he eventually entered into a sort of unofficial retirement and spent most of his time at home, reading, listening to the radio, writing letters to newspapers, and talking to Mrs. Taylor.

Sometimes, after completing breakfast, Mr. Taylor would get up, shave and bathe, dress, and go downstairs to his library to do what he called work. His work consisted usually of reading his mail, reading the daily papers, considering briefly his financial affairs, and then standing up, walking around the room, looking out the window at the garden, and perhaps rearranging the books on the shelves that ran along two entire walls of the room.

Somehow he could take an entire morning to complete such trivial matters and then it would be time for lunch. Once in a great while he and Mrs. Taylor would go out for lunch, driving primly into town in a very old automobile. They would eat quietly in a tearoom, then do a bit of shopping, and return home. But as the years passed, they appeared in the civic center more rarely. Most of the time they just stayed in the house, lunched together in the cozy kitchen, then sat in the parlor during the afternoon, or took naps or listened to the radio.

Mrs. Taylor's day consisted chiefly of housework. She did some crocheting, made jams and jellies, and twice a week would supervise the "heavy" work that was done by a colored girl named Althea, who had been serving them for over a decade.

In the afternoon Mrs. Taylor would often appear at the door of the library, and when Mr. Taylor would look up from his writing desk she would hold aloft the tray that held tea and cookies and say, "Is my little darling still working? We-e-elll, he had just better stop for a few minutes and put something into his little tum-tum."

After they had enjoyed a cup of tea, Mr. Taylor might take Mrs. Taylor on his lap and rest his head on her shoulder and say, "Thank you for da tea and da tookies."

He would have been terribly embarrassed, of course, to have been overheard speaking in such a manner. In public his mien was prim and solemn, but in the privacy of his home he luxuriated in the babying that his wife gave him. Once in a while Mrs. Taylor would forget herself in public and speak in her familiar singing, maternal way. At such times Mr. Taylor would frown and look away as if the woman with him were someone he did not know. His wife would make an apologetic face and the incident would be forgotten.

The Taylors had not always spoken to each other in this manner. For one thing, men always feel great embar-

rassment if they are caught speaking like children by someone whom they believe will disapprove of the practice. It
just happened that Mildred had always been given to the
custom of talking like a small child, and after a few years
the habit had more or less rubbed off on her husband. It
must be admitted, of course, that potentially the inclination existed within him or he would not have taken to it
so readily and so happily. It had begun, he thought, during their courtship, for though Mr. Taylor was shy he was
passionate and the discovery that he was loved by a remarkably uninhibited woman had released a great many
things in him that had always theretofore been bottled up.

It is not uncommon, as is well known, for lovers to
speak to each other in honeyed, unnatural tones, to bill and
coo as it were; and initially it is unlikely that the whispered
terms of endearment, the breathy infantile phrases with
which Mildred and Timothy addressed each other were in
any respect truly extraordinary. The thing was that they
took to the practice like ducks to water; and far from allowing it to die out, as is the case with most married couples,
they built it up till it colored practically all their discourse,
or at least that portion of it which took place between them
when they were alone.

After a few years Mrs. Taylor began to vary the breakfast menu. Coffee was replaced by cocoa and cereal was
substituted for the eggs. At first she served cold flake
cereal but after a time switched to hot, steaming oatmeals
and other grain mashes. One day, too, for a lark she put
a bib around Mr. Taylor's neck while serving him his
breakfast.

"My little baby boy," she said, "mustn't spill him's

cereal all over him's little chest. Mama will tie this little bib on her sloppy little boy."

They both had a good laugh over it and so every morning thereafter the bib became part of the ritual.

For a while Mr. Taylor took to tying it around his own neck, but this seemed somehow unsuitable and he eventually allowed Mrs. Taylor to resume the job.

When they were a bit younger Mrs. Taylor would occasionally remove the tray after breakfast and then climb into bed with her husband and the two would put their arms around each other and make love. With the passage of time, of course, this happened less often, but their physical interest in each other lasted rather longer than might be thought customary; and when it had finally disappeared almost altogether the Taylors hardly noticed because their love-making had always consisted largely of tender, baby-words and mother-child caresses and these they continued to employ.

Once in a great while, oddly enough, they would reverse roles. Now and then Mr. Taylor would adopt a mock manly voice, speaking in deep, throaty tones. "How's Daddy's little girl?" he would say. "How *is* my little baby girl?"

"I'm fine, Daddy," Mildred would say, pouting and looking sideways out of her eyes, like a child. "Do you wuv me?"

"Yes, I do," he would say, "I wuv you very much."

Then they would laugh and he would pull his wife down onto his lap and bounce her around and fondle her. "You *look* like my father," Mildred said once, speaking for a change in a normal tone. "You have the same blue eyes and the same small mouth. You look *just* like my father."

"But I don't want to be your father," Mr. Taylor said, slipping back into the infantile speech pattern. "I thought I was your little boy."

"Well, of course," Mrs. Taylor sang, "bwess his little heart. He *is* my little boy. He's dus' my little darling."

Earlier I believe I said the Taylors lived alone after the death of their child. Actually they had a dog at one time, but they only kept him for about a year. Mr. Taylor brought him home one day because he had found him on the street and felt sorry for him. Mrs. Taylor called him Bimbo, because that was the name of a dog she had owned years before; although after a few weeks she changed the name to Bimmy and finally to Timmy-Bimmy. She spoke to the dog as lovingly as she did to Mr. Taylor and after several months this got on Mr. Taylor's nerves. At the end of a year's time he took the dog to the city pound one day and had it done away with, then went home and told his wife he had been shopping and asked where the dog was. When she said she didn't know he went outside and pretended to look for it. After a few days Mrs. Taylor decided it was lost forever. She never wanted another one.

I do not want to give the impression that the Taylors' life was one long, uninterrupted session of prattling. They had their disagreements, as do all couples, and upon very rare occasions could be quite testy with each other. Now and then it was not unknown for Mr. Taylor to shout at his wife and for her to burst into tears. But, luckily enough, these arguments were always followed by weepy reconciliations, at which times the talk would be more syrupy than ever and at which times also, at least during the earlier years of their marriage, their physical passion for each other would be quite vigorous.

Most of the time Mr. Taylor was quite content to follow his wife's direction, for it relieved him of the responsibility of making important decisions and gave him a sort of security. Consequently, occasions for disagreement were few and far between.

One time when Mr. Taylor had to go to Philadelphia to confer with his lawyers, he returned, after an absence of two days, to find a carpenter picking up some tools on the front porch.

Nodding politely, Mr. Taylor stepped into the vestibule and hung up his hat and coat.

"Mildred," he called.

"I'm up here," she said, from the head of the stairs. "Has the man left yet?"

"Yes," Mr. Taylor said. "What was he doing?"

"You'll see," his wife said. "I have a surprise for you."

He walked upstairs and looked at the blank doors to the various rooms.

"Where are you?" he said.

"I'm in here," she said, speaking from their bedroom.

When he walked in and saw what the surprise was, he had to admit that it was a surprise.

"Well, well," he said, stepping around the bed. "Well, well, well."

Mrs. Taylor came to him and put her arms around his neck.

"It's something for my little darling," she said. "I know you'll think I was extravagant, but it didn't cost much really. I thought it would make you laugh."

"It did," said Mr. Taylor. "That is, I didn't laugh but it is funny." Then his blood froze. "Good God," he said. "What must the carpenter think?"

"I was very clever," Mrs. Taylor said. "He's not from around here at all. I mean I called him in because he works on the other side of town and doesn't know us from Adam. We'll never see or hear from him again, so what does it matter what he thinks?"

"I suppose you're right," he said.

"Take off your clothes," Mrs. Taylor said.

"What?"

"You're not going to do anything else today. It's almost dinnertime anyway. Take off your clothes and put on your little pajamas. Mama wants to see her baby boy in his little bed."

"All wite," Mr. Taylor said, hanging up his jacket.

Outside it began to rain.

"Just got home in time," Mr. Taylor said, taking off his pants. Lightning flickered against the windows and there was heard the distant grumble of thunder. After Mr. Taylor got into his pajamas he put on an old blue terry-cloth robe and they went downstairs to have dinner. Mrs. Taylor served red wine with the meal and then sat down and looked out the window sadly.

"What's the matter?" said Mr. Taylor.

"I don't like rainstorms," Mrs. Taylor said. "They make me think of—you know——"

Mr. Taylor knew. She meant the baby. The dear lost dead baby. He had caught cold playing in the rain and had died four days later of pneumonia.

They had another glass of wine. After dinner they sat in the parlor for a while, then went back upstairs and Mr. Taylor looked at the bed again.

"My, my," he said. "That is really something."

"I don't think you need give another thought to the

carpenter," Mrs. Taylor said. "After all, it could be for an invalid."

"That's true," said Mr. Taylor. "I hadn't thought of that."

"Well," she said, "are you ready to go to bed?"

"I suppose so," he said. "I'm pretty tired after the train ride."

"All right," she said, sliding a chair next to the bed. "Climb in. I'll go downstairs and fix us a nice hot pot of cocoa."

When she had left, Mr. Taylor got up on the chair and gingerly lifted one leg up over the bars that Mrs. Taylor had had built along the side of his bed. Then he drew the other leg in and stretched out. The carpenter had done a good job. It looked remarkably like a baby's crib. Bigger, of course.

He lay there for perhaps ten minutes and then his wife walked in the room. She looked as if she had been crying and she was holding something behind her.

"Bring the cocoa?" Mr. Taylor said.

"Yes," she said. "I have it right here." From behind her she drew a baby's bottle, full of hot chocolate milk.

"Where did you get that?" he said.

"I bought it this afternoon," she said. "For my little darling." She came over to the crib and inserted the nipple of the bottle neatly between his teeth. He sucked at it tentatively.

"Is it all right?" she asked tenderly.

"Mmmm-mmmm," he said, in the affirmative. Suddenly he felt good. It did not seem like a game. It seemed to Timothy that he really *was* an infant again. He tried squinting his eyes, holding them almost closed, to see if he could make Mildred's face appear to be the face of his mother. He could. Taking the bottle out of his mouth, he pouted and frowned.

"What's da mattuh with my little angel?" Mrs. Taylor said, laughing but with tears in her eyes.

"I'm cold," Timothy said.

"Is he?" Mrs. Taylor said. "Is dat little baby cold? Well, we'll just have to do something about that, won't we?" Walking to the linen closet, she withdrew a blanket and carried it to the crib.

"There," she said, tucking it around him. "Dat'll keep my little angel nice and warm."

"You'll have to let Althea go," Mr. Taylor said.

"Yes," she answered. "I know."

Without Althea Mrs. Taylor found it rather difficult to keep the house in spotless order, and after a time the gentle rottenness that the building seemed to exude from the outside crept inside, too, and hid in the furniture and the drapes and the rugs. The Taylors did not notice it themselves because it came as gradually and as stealthily as age, but over a period of time the house became a musty, dismal place.

Mr. Taylor finally took to staying in his crib till noon and eating nothing but baby foods. This made him lose weight and gave him trouble with his teeth, and when Mildred noticed the hollowness of his cheeks she worried about him. Her solicitude increased and she finally made with her own hands several pairs of sleepers for him, of warm light blue flannel, with the feet sewn right in. One day when she was in the back yard watering the flowers, Mr. Taylor's brother and Mr. Taylor's attorney came to the front door to see Timothy because he had not answered his mail nor his phone for several months. Receiving no answer to their knocking, they walked in, looked about the first floor, then proceeded upstairs. When they walked into Timothy's bedroom he was lying in the crib in his light blue flannel pajamas, sucking on a bottle of warm milk.

His brother walked over to the crib and looked down at Timothy, white-faced.

"What's the matter, Tim?" he said, softly. "Why are you lying here like this?"

Timothy smiled gently and a trickle of milk ran down his chin.

4

The Secret

I DIDN'T know I was dead until I walked into the bathroom and looked in the mirror.

In fact I didn't even know it at that exact moment. The only thing I knew for sure then was that I couldn't see anything in the mirror except the wallpaper behind me and the small table with the hairbrushes on it low against the wall.

I think I just stood there for perhaps ten seconds. Then I reached out and tried to touch the mirror, because I thought I was still asleep on the couch in the den and I figured that if I moved around a bit, so to speak, in my dream I could sort of jar myself awake. I know it isn't a very logical way to think, but in moments of stress we all do unusual things.

The first moment I really knew I was dead was when I couldn't feel the mirror. I couldn't even see the hand

I had stretched out to touch it. That's when I knew there was nothing physical about me. I had identity, I was conscious, but I was invisible. I knew then I had to be either dead or a raving maniac.

Just to be sure, I stepped back into the den. I felt better when I saw my body lying on the couch. I guess that sounds like a peculiar thing to say too, but what I mean is, I'd rather be dead than insane. Maybe *you* wouldn't but that's what makes horse races.

My next sensation (that's the only word I can think of to convey my meaning to you) was that there was something pressing on my mind, some nagging matter I had almost forgotten. It was very much like the feeling you sometimes have when you walk over to a bookshelf or a clothes closet, let's say, and then suddenly just stand there and say to yourself, "Now why did I come over here?" I felt a bit as if I had an imminent appointment.

I went over to the couch and looked down at myself. The magazine was open on the floor where it had slipped from my hand, and my right foot had fallen down as if I might have been making an effort to get up when I died.

It must have been the round of golf that did it. Larkin had warned me about exertion as long as three years ago, but after a fearful six months I had gotten steadily more overconfident. I was physically big, robust, muscular. I had played football at college. Inactivity annoyed the hell out of me. I remembered the headache that had plagued me over the last three holes, the feeling of utter weariness in the locker room after the game. But the cold shower had refreshed me a bit and a drink had relaxed me. I felt pretty good when I got home, except for an inner weariness and a lingering trace of the headache.

It had come while I was asleep, that's why I didn't recognize it. I mean if it comes in the form of a death-bed scene, with people standing around you shaking their heads, or if comes in the form of a bullet from an angry gun, or in the form of drowning, well, it certainly comes as no surprise. But it came to me while I was lying there asleep in the den after reading a magazine. What with the sun and the exercise and the drink, I was a little groggy anyway and my dreams were sort of wild and confused. Naturally when I found myself standing in front of the mirror I thought it was all just another part of a dream.

It wasn't, of course. You know that. You do if you read the papers, anyway, because they played it up pretty big on page one. "Westchester Man 'Dead' for 16 Minutes." That was the headline in the *Herald Tribune*. In the Chicago *Daily News* the headline on the story was "New Yorker 'Dead,' Revived by Doctors." Notice those quotation marks around the word *dead*. That's always the way the papers handle it. I say always because it happens all the time. Last year alone there were nine of us around the country. Ask any of us about it and we'll just laugh good-naturedly and tell you that papers were right, we weren't dead. Of course we'll tell you that. What else could we tell you?

So there I was, beside the couch, staring down at myself. I remember looking around the room, but I was alone. They hadn't come yet. I felt a flicker of some kind that would be hard to describe—an urgency, an anxiety, a realization that I had left a few things undone. Then I tried a ridiculous thing. I tried to get back into myself. But it wouldn't work. I couldn't do it alone.

Jo would have to help, although we had just had a

bitter argument. She had been in the kitchen when I had gone in to take a nap. I hurried to the kitchen. She was still there. Shelling peas, I think, and talking to the cook. "Jo," I said, but of course she couldn't hear me. I moved close to her and tried to tell her. I felt like a dog trying to interest a distracted master.

"Agnes," she said, "would you please close the window."

That's all she said. Then she stood up, wiped her hands, and walked out of the kitchen and down the hall to the den. I don't know how I did it, but in a vague way she had gotten the message.

She let out a tiny scream when she saw the color of my face. Then she shook me twice and then she said, "Oh, my God," and started to cry, quietly. She did not go to pieces. Thank God she didn't go to pieces or I wouldn't be able to tell the tale today.

Still crying, she ran to the hall phone and called Larkin. He ordered an ambulance and met it at the house inside of ten minutes. In all, only twelve minutes had elapsed since I had tried to look at myself in the mirror.

I remember Larkin came in on the run without talking. He ran past me as I stood at the door of the den and knelt down beside my body on the couch.

"When did you find him?" he said.

"Ten minutes ago," Jo said.

He took something out of his bag and injected the body with adrenalin, and then they bundled "me" off to the hospital. I followed. It was five minutes away.

I never would have believed a crew could work so fast. Oxygen. More adrenalin. And then one of the doctors pushed a button and the table my body was on began to lift slowly, first at one end and then at the other, like a slow teeter-totter.

"Watch for blood pressure," Larkin whispered to an assistant, who squeezed a rubber bulb.

I was so fascinated watching them I did not at first realize I had visitors.

"Interesting," a voice said.

"Yes," I answered, without consciously directing my attention away from the body on the tilting table. Then I felt at one and the same time a pang of fear and the release of the nagging anxiety that had troubled me earlier.

I must have been expecting them. There was one on each side of me.

The second one looked at the body, then at Larkin and the others. "Do you think they'll succeed?" he said.

"I don't know," I said. "I hope so."

The answer seemed significant. The two looked at each other.

"We must be very certain," he said. "Would it matter so much to you either way?"

"Why, yes," I said. "I suppose it would. I mean, there's work I've left unfinished."

"Work isn't important *now*, is it?" asked the first one.

"No," I agreed. "It isn't. But there are other things. Things I have to do for Jo. For the children."

Again the two seemed to confer, silently.

"What sort of things?"

"Oh," I said, "there are some business details I've left up in the air. There'll be legal trouble, I'm sure, about the distribution of the assets of my firm."

"Is that all?" the first one said, coming closer to me.

Larkin began to shake his head slowly. He looked as if he were losing hope.

Then I thought of something else. "You'll laugh," I said, "but something silly just came into my mind."

"What is it?" asked the second one.

"I would like to apologize to Jo," I said, "because we had an argument this afternoon. I'd forgotten I'd promised to take her and the children out to dinner and a movie. We had an argument about it. I suppose it sounds ridiculous at a time like this to talk about something that may seem so trivial, but that's what I'd like to do. I'd like to apologize to her for the things I said, and I'd like to keep that date. I'd like to take the children to see that movie, even if it is some cowboys-and-Indians thing that'll bore the hell out of me."

That's when it all began to happen. I can't say that suddenly the two were gone. To say *I* was gone would be more to the point. They didn't leave me. I left them. I was still unconscious, but now I was on the table. I was back inside my head. I was dreaming and I was dizzy. I didn't know what was happening in the room then, of course. I didn't know anything till later that night when I woke up. I felt weak and shaky and for a few minutes I wasn't aware that Larkin and some other doctors and Jo were standing around my bed. There was some kind of an oxygen tent over my chest and head, and my mouth felt dry and stiff. My tongue was like a piece of wood but I was alive. And I could see Jo. She looked tired and wan but she looked mighty beautiful to me.

The next day the men from the papers came around and interviewed me. They wrote that I was in good spirits and was sitting up in bed swapping jokes with the nurses, which was something of an exaggeration.

It was almost a month before I could keep that date with Jo and the kids, and by that time the picture wasn't even playing in our neighborhood. We had to drive all the way over to Claremont to see it, but we stopped at a nice tearoom on the way and had a wonderful dinner.

People still ask me what I felt while I was "dead." They always say it just that way, getting quotation marks into their voices, treating it as something a little bit amusing, the way the newspapers did. And I go along with it, of course. You can't say to them, "Why, yes, I was dead." They'd lock you up.

Funny thing about it all was that I'd always been more or less afraid of the idea of death. But after dying, I wasn't. I always knew I'd eventually go again, but it never worried me. I did my best to make a go of my relationships with other people and that was about the size of it. One other thing I did was write this little story and give it to a friend of mine, to be published only after my death.

If you're reading it, that means I've gone again. But this time I won't be back.

5

The Martyrs

*The following story was suggested by an article in
Life magazine which told of the disaster that struck a
party of American missionaries in the unexplored
jungle of South America.*

Our people will long remember the
brave and unselfish labors of the missionaries whose bodies
were found last summer by a search party high in the upper
ranges of the mountains of the last frontier.

Among the effects found by the searchers was a diary
that had been faithfully kept by Father Zalé. Herewith we
print excerpts from that diary. The Zalé account begins
by describing the trip into the wilderness.

First entry: Last night as we came within sight of the
mountain range that our maps had told us about we all

knelt briefly to give thanks to the Almighty. All, that is, except our pilot, Quanto, who kept his eyes on the instrument panel but who nevertheless joined in the prayer wholeheartedly.

For a long time we had debated amongst ourselves as to the best time to make the trip, and finally, the decision having been made that it was the Lord's time to try to contact the savages, we had taken off, full of both fear and confidence, but calm in the assurance that since we were doing the work of the heavenly Father our mission could not come to ill.

It was one morning shortly after dawn that we actually saw the mountain range. Our hearts leaped up at the sight of the massive purple peaks, their tops glistening in the brilliant morning light.

I spoke to Quanto as we circled, looking for a suitable landing place, and we discussed again the wisdom of having made our departure secretly and without the knowledge of our townspeople. It had been our fear that if the authorities knew we were going into the forbidden area at this particular time they might have either tried to stop us, or else, what would have been worse, attempted to send an armed party with us. Thus, we feared, there might have been the danger of a clash with the natives, with the result that the missionary movement could have been set back for many years.

We had selected this particular area for our experiment in contacting these strange people because of its isolation and because our earliest explorers had told us that it was one of the few places where the natives had literally no contact with surrounding tribes for many months at a time. Hence we believed we could approach them in love and innocence without the fear that their original apprehension might be communicated to nearby areas and our plans therefore frustrated.

Within minutes after sighting the mountains we found a suitable landing place, a river-valley clearing where there were not many trees.

Climbing stiffly from our craft we fell to the ground and praised God for our safe arrival. After breakfasting we slept briefly, for the trip had been exhausting.

Second entry: It has now been three days since we landed in this desolate but strangely beautiful spot and we have yet to see any sign of life, except a few strange wild animals unlike any we have observed heretofore.

Third entry: Quanto and the others scouted the nearby terrain this morning while I stood guard over our ship. They carried with them ribbons and brightly colored discs for use as gifts to indicate to the natives that our motives are friendly. I sat for a long time by the river, in the shade of a large tree, reading the Scriptures. At length the party returned, having failed to make contact with any of the inhabitants of this forbidding land.

Fourth entry: At last the Lord has blessed us! This afternoon while we were preparing a meal over a fire, the bushes parted across the river and we had our first look full into a native's face. For a short period of time he stood motionless and then slowly he raised his arms and we saw that he was carrying a metal weapon. We smiled and waved our hands to show that we were friendly and unarmed and after a moment he lowered his shaft, continuing, however, to regard us warily. I rose and started to walk slowly toward the river, smiling the while, but at my approach the poor devil evidently became alarmed, for he retreated with great haste into the brush. Quanto suggested that we follow slowly in the direction of the man's flight and this we immediately agreed to do, for we thought that the native's first desire would be to return to his fellows and that if we therefore followed him we might have some idea as to the location of the village that we had so far been unable to find.

We walked across the shallow stream and set out in pursuit of the man we had seen, catching sight of him from time to time as the foliage ahead thinned. Within a few minutes, sad to say, he had outdistanced us or had taken hidden refuge, for we lost sight of him and did not thereafter know what course to take. We pressed on for a short distance until we came to a clearing from which led a faintly discernible path. Evidently the man or his fellows were accustomed to pass this way from time to time, so we left a few small gifts to indicate our good faith and returned to our camp without further incident.

Fifth entry: This day we returned to the spot and discovered that our gifts had been picked up. Praise God! The people now must know we are their friends.

Sixth entry: We feel we are being watched. Last night there were new sounds in the brush across the river and once or twice we thought we saw a flickering light in the trees.

Seventh entry: One grows impatient to do the Lord's work but the Lord is not mindful of time. We must be patient.

Eighth entry: This morning when we awakened we found we were being observed from across the stream by a band of eight natives, all men. They were lightly clad, armed, and unsmiling. Again we greeted them pleasantly, after which Quanto walked bravely across the river holding two boxes of gifts under his arm, displaying his hands the while to show that he was concealing no weapons. Setting the boxes down on the sand he retreated to our side, saying in a loud voice, "We like you. We are friendly. See? We smile. Look in the boxes. We bring gifts." But of course they could not understand our language and we could not be sure that they correctly read our intentions.

One of the men approached the boxes warily and kicked at it with his toe, tipping it and spilling the contents out onto the sand. We had enclosed a vest, a copy of the Scriptures, a few coins, and a small knife to indicate that we would even be willing to put a weapon into their hands by way of proving our trust and lack of guile. The man knelt slowly, picked up the knife and the Scriptures, and then withdrew, walking backward.

When he had rejoined his companions they conferred briefly and then departed.

Ninth entry: This is a great day for the advance of the Lord's work. Quanto was at one end of the landing strip, I at the other, and the rest of our party were bathing when suddenly from directly across the river three natives walked out of the brush and advanced toward the water, talking loudly. We gathered together in a knot and smiled, making gestures of welcome. The Lord be praised, they evidently correctly interpreted our signs for they walked boldly into the water and waded toward our side of the stream.

A little past the middle they paused and at this moment I waded out to meet them, smiling and hand outstretched. The smallest of the three seemed wary, but I decided to act with initiative in the full confidence of the Lord and so stepped forward and took the man's hand in my own, pointing to our side of the stream as if to say, "Come, join us." After a moment's hesitation he allowed himself to be pulled in our direction and then the three of them smiled and we all walked together to dry sand.

The three men were wearing heavy knee-high waterproof boots which interested us greatly and we all spent the first few minutes examining each other's attire. Finally the tallest of the natives indicated that he wanted to approach "The Silver Lady" and with a glance at Quanto I indicated approval. By gestures he seemed to be saying that he wanted to make a flight, so we talked it over and decided that it would be a good thing. Quanto took him up for a short trip while his companions watched openmouthed. When they had landed the man walked out and bounded over to his fellows jabbering to them about the marvel he had just experienced.

They then made signs of gratitude and, smiling broadly, retreated.

Tenth entry: Our labors are bearing fruit. We have been here now for many days and are making good progress in learning the spoken tongue of these strange people and have even succeeded in teaching them a few of our words. Also by sign language we are able to exchange simple ideas with reasonable ease.

Eleventh entry: We have now met many natives and although some seem unfriendly, most of them, I believe, are trustworthy. The females continue to regard us with some suspicion.

Twelfth entry: We have begun to speak of the Lord and His heavenly message. These people seem fascinated by what we are telling them.

Thirteenth entry: Have now for a considerable length of time spoken of the Lord's message. The women seem to resent what we say, but the men are curious and attentive. Yesterday there was an argument among the natives but it was conducted at some distance from us and we could not clearly understand what they were saying. Will go now to eat the noonday meal and enjoy a short sleep.

This note, apparently the last that Father Zalé wrote, gives perhaps a small clue to the method of the disaster. It is possible that the party was resting after the middle-of-the-day meal when it was attacked.

When a long time later a search party landed in the clearing, Zalé's mutilated body was found face down at the water's edge, Quanto was sprawled lifeless near his ship, and the others were either dead or missing.

The method of killing was interesting. We found small metal pellets imbedded in all of the bodies. Evidently, despite their discoveries and advances in the application of atomic energy, the people of this planet were still using ancient methods of weapon construction. Quanto's hands were still wrapped around the shaft of the weapon that had killed him. The peculiar word "Winchester" was engraved in its side. Zalé's entry book included, in addition to the above formal notations, a number of jottings and scribblings, one of which told us that the natives called their country "Montana."

What a tragic pity it is that these savage people took the lives of those who came among them only to bring them the message of the one true faith. Ah, well. Always, after the missionaries, the soldiers.

6

Point of View

After the word had gotten around town that the child's body had been found just off the main highway about a mile from Roy Davis' gas station, there were three or four people who remembered having seen *something* lying in the weeds off to the left of the road.

"I distinctly recollect," said Buddy Elder, "seeing some cloth or something or other as I drove in yesterday afternoon. Didn't stop, though."

"Wouldn't-a done any good if you had," someone said. "Kid was dead then twenty-four hours."

It was three days later that the sheriff picked up Lafe Washington as he lay drunk in his shack. Lafe was never too bright and he had been walking around town with the child's change purse practically in plain sight in his khaki shirt pocket, half-drunk and talking to himself.

When they went to pick him up they found a blood-stained pair of denim trousers hanging on a nail.

Some of the white people of the town, what with it being Saturday night and there being nothing much to do but relax and drink and smolder, got into a rather ugly mood. There was even some talk of going down to the jail and dragging Lafe out. The colored people, too, surprisingly enough, began to mutter. In years past they would have kept their own counsel and never dreamed of concerning themselves with civic vengeance, but this particular crime had aroused an uncommon degree of hatred.

It was not acceptable to the people of the valley that any man should kill any child, and for once white and colored alike were seething, although not to an equal degree. There seemed no question in anyone's mind about Lafe Washington's guilt; the few who did have qualms were relieved when early Monday morning it was announced that Lafe had made a full confession.

"Ah don' know why ah did it," he said, "but she gimme some sass, Mistuh Sheriff, and ah jus' hit huh. She started cryin' and then ah hit huh again." There were other details too sordid to relate, although for all that one was afraid to offend the sensibilities of the people Lafe might have recited them aloud to music in the town square; within twenty-four hours the details of the crime, horrible as they were, were exaggerated, blown up out of all relation to reality, almost savored over.

Monday morning the town was astonished to learn that Lafe Washington, who would scarcely have been thought to have the gumption, had escaped from jail.

When the news reached Gus Benton late that afternoon, he turned to the men around him and said, "Like to get my hands on the son-of-a-bitch. String him up's what I'd like to do."

"You ain't just a-woofin'," responded Martin Cole. "That would really be somethin' to do. That would show them bastards once and for all to keep their hands off our kind."

"Yeah," said Gus drawlingly. "Be a good lesson to all of 'em."

"You guys are nuts," said Sanford Davis, a small man and a careful one. "You ain't got no right to lay a hand on Washington. Two wrongs don't make a right."

" 'f that was your kid you wouldn't say that," Gus said. "You didn't see that child. I did. She didn't look so good."

"Well, don't get yourself all riled up, boy," Sanford said. "There ain't been no lynchin' 'round here for over twenty years and I don't figure they be one now."

"What you mean?" demanded Gus. "They been two in Georgia during the past——"

"I'm not talkin' 'bout the whole *state*," said Sanford. "I mean right here 'round the valley."

"You don't know *what* you talkin' about," Gus said.

The three men got in the battered Ford pickup that was owned by the lumber company Sanford worked for, and started on the road to Ludlow. Gus had a bottle and the three of them passed it around. About ten minutes out of town they came to a group of cars pulled over to the side of the road.

"Slow down," Martin said. "That's the sheriff."

A khaki-clad figure stood almost in the middle of the road, one hand upraised. When the truck stopped he walked over and put one foot on the running board.

"We're lookin' for Washington," he said quietly. "Heard

he'd been seen through here. You boys see anything along the road as you came up?"

"No, sir," Gus said. "We'd like to, but we didn't see nothin'."

Another man walked up beside the sheriff. "He's somewhere between here and Ludlow," the man said. "You can be pretty sure of that. He wouldn't be back this way."

"I guess you're right," the sheriff said. "All right, let's fan out along this side of the road. We've got about two hours before it gets dark. If we don't find him we can come back tomorrow and try the other side."

When the two men stepped away from the truck Sanford gunned the engine.

"Where you goin'?" Gus said.

"Where you think?" Sanford said.

"Hold on," Gus said. "I wonder if they could use some help here."

"They don't need the likes of us," Martin said. "Let's keep movin'."

They sat silently for a moment, watching the sheriff as he moved away.

"There's twelve of us," he was saying to the man at his side. "That's not enough, but it'll have to do. Now remember—if there's any gunplay I'll handle that part of it. We just want all these men to fan out and beat the bushes. No telling where the bastard might be hiding."

"You hear that?" Gus said.

"Yeah," Martin said. "What about it?"

"There's gonna be some action around here for sure. Let's wait till they start out and then follow 'em. See if we can do any good."

"They don't want us," Martin said.

After a moment it seemed that the sheriff's men had all struck off into the brush. "Come on," Gus said to Sanford. "Pull over to the side. We got work to do."

Sanford eased the truck off the road and turned off the motor with only slight reluctance. The three men felt a nervousness in the stomach. Each of them wondered what he would do if he met Lafe in the woods.

"Lafe got a gun?" Sanford said.

"No," said a man who had walked up behind them, unheard. They whirled in embarrassment.

"You boys keep your eyes open," the man said as he turned off the road. "He's not armed but he's still dangerous." They watched his blue jacket moving away.

When the man had disappeared Sanford said, "Well? Let's go if we're goin'."

They shuffled off into the weeds at the side of the highway, where the ground dropped away from the cracked asphalt.

"Whoo-wee," Gus said. "I'd like to be the one to find that son-of-a-bitch. I'd fix him."

"You better shut up," Sanford said. "You're lookin' for trouble."

"Sure I'm lookin' for trouble," Gus said. "What you think we lookin' for? A Sunday-school picnic? I tell you, man, that kid had her little dress torn off and she was cut up bad. She's your kid you'd sure be singin' outta the other side your mouth."

"I'd like to get *my* hands on him," Martin said. "There's too many people 'round here need a lesson anyway. Might do some good to get this goddamned Washington. Might show people a thing or two."

"Boy," said Sanford, "you're talkin' crazy."

Keeping their eye on the man in the blue jacket, they moved off through the woods, spreading out so that there was a distance of about fifty feet between them. Sanford was on the left, Gus in the center, Martin on the right.

Once, about twenty minutes after they had lost sight of the highway, something moved in the brush, and the three stiffened, listening.

"Must have been a rabbit," Sanford whispered hoarsely after a moment.

"Yeah," Gus said. He was disappointed. The woods began to look confusing to him. "Martin," he called, "you still see that guy the other side of you?"

"Yes," Martin said. "Not every minute, but I pick him up from time to time."

"Don't lose him," Gus said. "I wouldn't wanna have any trouble findin' my way back outta here."

"No problem," Martin said. "The road is just off to the right here a ways."

"Yeah," said Gus, "but it makes a right turn about a mile down and if we don't turn with it we gone be walkin' into some mighty deep timber."

Half an hour later Gus said, "Let's rest a minute."

"All right," Martin said.

"You still hear the rest of 'em?" Sanford asked, wiping his brow. He was unfamiliar with the back woods.

"No," Martin said, "but we're all right. We'll catch up."

"I'm pooped," Gus said, taking the pint from his jacket pocket. They passed the bottle around twice and then started walking again. After a few minutes Martin realized they were lost.

"Hey, man," he said to Gus, "I ain't see that fella in the blue jacket for about twenty minutes or so."

"Son-of-a-bitch," Gus said. "So we *are* lost. Damn, I shoulda worked that side myself."

They gathered together in a small, worried knot and looked for the sun but it had gone down, though there was still plenty of daylight.

"Boy," said Gus in agonized frustration, "I'd like to get my hands on that Washington now. Wasn't for him I'd be home now, havin' dinner."

"Me too," Martin said. "Like to kill the bastard."

"You ever seen anybody killed?" Sanford said.

"Seen 'em?" Gus said. "Man, I've killed 'em. I fought in Italy for twenty-three months. Killin' a guy ain't nothin'. Besides"—he spat out of the side of his mouth—"you forgettin' that Washington done whatever killin's been done around here. Whatever happens to him from here on in he's got comin' to him."

Sanford took another drink from the bottle that Gus had passed to him. "I guess you're right in a way," he said. He began to think of his own child, a nine-year-old boy. If anybody ever laid a hand on Billy, Sanford considered, he would be quite willing to commit murder. The alcohol began to warm up his brain and give him confidence. He no longer felt apprehensive about meeting Lafe Washington. Suddenly he knew he *hoped* to meet him. He passed the bottle on to Martin, who emptied it, then returned it to Gus somewhat apologetically. Gus threw it into the brush, swearing.

It was then that they saw Lafe Washington standing quietly, looking at them, beside a large tree.

For ten seconds nobody spoke or moved.

Then without a word Lafe broke and ran, disappearing into the brush. They took after him, trotting unsteadily.

"He didn't have no gun, did he?" Sanford said.

"No," Gus said, his lips turned down. "Don't you remember what the man said?"

"How we gonna bring him in?" Martin said.

"I don't know," Gus said. "All we gotta do now is catch the mother."

It was not difficult to keep on Washington's trail. They could easily hear him pounding through the trees, falling, breathing heavily, breaking twigs and small branches.

"Stop, you son-of-a-bitch," Gus called out.

They were surprised to hear Lafe cry out, "You leave me alone!"

"Ha!" said Gus. "We gettin' him now!"

For several more minutes the four staggered through the forest till at last Washington had a lead of only ten yards. From time to time they could clearly see his face, turned backward, the eyes flashing fear, the mouth wide.

"You *better* run, you murderin'——" Gus shouted.

Lafe stumbled into a tree, dropped, rose, and began to run again, wobblingly. Gus was now almost upon him, with Martin and Sanford not far behind.

With a desperate spurt of energy Gus closed the short gap between himself and Lafe and leaped upon the latter's back. The two fell heavily to the ground. Lafe rose but just in time to take a punch in the face from Martin. As he fell Sanford kicked him in the ribs and he whimpered.

"There!" shouted Sanford, thinking that all the fight was out of Lafe, but Washington suddenly lashed out with both feet and kicked him in the groin. Sanford doubled up, screaming with pain. "Ohhh," he shrieked, "God damn you!"

Gus, who had by now regained his feet, lunged at

Lafe, knocked him off balance, and kicked him as he fell. Sanford began stomping on him as he lay thrashing in panic on the ground, and then Gus ran and picked up a skull-sized rock that was partly embedded in the loose earth at the foot of a tree.

"Ye get away from me," Lafe shouted. "Ah didn't mean to kill that little nigger."

The last thing Lafe Washington ever expected to see on this earth, as he sat white-faced on the ground, blue eyes rolling, blond hair matted to his bleeding forehead, was three strange Negroes coming at him with murder in their eyes, one of them holding aloft a heavy rock.

But that was the last thing he saw on this earth.

7

The Award

CLARE walked up to my desk with a long face.

"What's the good word?" I said, trying to be cheerful.

"Read it and weep," she said, handing me a letter. It was from Marty Davis.

"Dear Harry," the letter said. "Thank you for your letter of February 14 and for the kind invitation you extended to Bob and myself. He is extremely flattered, naturally, that your organization should choose to name him Mr. Entertainment for the year, but unfortunately he will be making a film in Japan this spring and we will all be leaving for Tokyo early in April, which means he couldn't attend your banquet in New York on April 27."

I didn't bother to read any further.

"Well," I said. "Two down. Where do we go from here?"

"I don't know," Clare said. "I thought sure Gleason would be able to do it or I would have gotten the letter off to Hope a long time ago."

"What's that got to do with it?" I said.

"Nothing," she said, "except Jackie giving us the bad news so late made us lose three valuable weeks."

"I am hip," I said, "but don't worry. We've done it before and we can do it again."

"I don't know," she said. "It gets harder every year . . . comedians moving to the Coast and all. Why the hell do they go through this rigmarole anyway? Why don't people just send in their money, period?"

"Hush," I said. "You start talking like that and we'll be out of work."

You see, Clare and I are partners in a very fascinating business: fund-raising. The average organization doesn't know beans about raising money, so they call in specialists. That's us. We're set up to handle the entire operation: organize lunches, dances, benefits, banquets, telephone appeals, direct-mail campaigns—you know, the whole business. We work on a very modest percentage, although some of our colleagues work on flat salary. But either way I'm sure you'll agree there's nothing unethical about it. The money goes to charity and everybody's happy.

Except that six years ago, wanting to make a good impression when we signed on this particular account, Clare and I decided to kick up some dust and get a little newspaper and newsreel attention by holding a lush banquet at the Waldorf and passing out Citations of Merit to some big show-business names.

It's a good dodge and I must admit we didn't invent it. The actors are a push-over, of course. Just tell them they've

won an award and they jump at the bait. Then we charge
fifty or a hundred bucks a plate and the cash customers
pour in, as much to gawk at the celebrities as to help the
organization. As I said before, it's all for sweet charity,
and for a long time it's been running like clockwork.

Lately, though, it's been getting tough to line up top-
drawer names. About three years ago we put ourselves
out on a limb by naming Groucho Marx as Mr. Entertainment, as he was a smash. Got a million laughs at the dinner,
was quoted in everybody's column, and attracted a lot of
attention to the organization, which of course is what Clare
and I are most interested in. The next year, naturally, we
had to get somebody more or less as big as Groucho so we
invited Arthur Godfrey. But he wasn't having any. He
sent us a nice check, and frankly I've never been so dis-
gusted by a large contribution. Money we can get pretty
easily these days. It was a big drawing card for our banquet
that we really needed, and when Arthur turned us down
I began to worry a little. Next we tried Sid Caesar, but
when Sid found out he would have to make a speech of
acceptance he, too, begged off because he only does bits
and sketches and doesn't like to talk in public "as himself,"
as they say in the trade.

We finally got somebody, of course, and everything
worked out fine. But each year it's been getting tougher.
Last year we had to go through Berle, Gobel, Skelton, and
Garry Moore before we pinned somebody down. And to
tell you the truth, I think some of these guy have a lot
of nerve saying no to us. After all, they're being honored
by a great organization with thousands of contributing
members and some mighty imposing names on the letter-

head. It's true that there's no voting or anything—Clare and I, we just pick the names ourselves—but, even so, it's a big thing. We send them a wire first:

I AM PLEASED TO INFORM YOU THAT OUR ORGANIZA-
TION HAS JUST NAMED YOU MR. ENTERTAINMENT OF
1956 FOR THE GENERAL EXCELLENCE OF YOUR TELE-
VISION PERFORMANCES DURING THE PAST YEAR.

It has to be television, by the way. Movies or radio or records don't mean a thing in connection with a deal like this. The guy has to be working in television.

PLEASE ACCEPT MY PERSONAL CONGRATULATIONS.
DETAILS CONCERNING FORMAL PRESENTATION OF YOUR
AWARD SUPPLIED IN LETTER TO FOLLOW.

We send the wire out over the signature of our honorary president, you understand, who is always somebody mighty important. We've had General MacArthur, Oscar Hammerstein, and Governor Dewey, just to give you an idea. Naturally, being busy men, they don't have the time to handle any of the details of their office, so what they're actually doing is just allowing us to use their names. Like if you were to get a wire from me, Harry Slater, you'd probably throw it away, but getting a wire signed General Sarnoff or Herbert Hoover, you sit up and take notice.

We send out three copies of this wire. One to the guy himself, one to his agent or manager, and one to his publicity man. Usually it does the trick, or anyway it did up until recently when some of the boys began playing hard to get. If we get a turn-down we make a few quick phone calls, tell 'em to keep our correspondence confidential, and then start all over again with some other target. But, as I say, I think some of these guys have a lot of nerve saying no to us. A lot of them say they can't fly in from the Coast, that they're busy doing their shows every week, and so on, but if a guy really wants to make a trip he'll do it. Groucho had flown in from the Coast, although it's true his show is on film and he has more free time than the guys who work live. Also he had to come here anyway to do a show for Max Liebman, and our timing just happened to be lucky.

So anyway, here we were, Clare and I, with rejection slips from Hope and Gleason, and banquet time rushing in on us like the Notre Dame forward wall.

"Comedians are getting tough," I said. "What about singers. How does Perry Como strike you?"

"It would be a pleasure," Clare said.

"Cut the comedy," I said. "Do you think he'd go for it?"

"I don't know," she said. "What about the speech bit?"

"He's not a cretin," I said. "He can talk."

"But he strikes me as the kind who doesn't like to," she said.

Clare's a better judge of human nature than I am so I didn't argue with her. She takes care of the subtler problems we run up against, and handles a lot of the detail work. I like to tell myself that I do the big thinking for the two of us.

"He could sing," I said.

"All right. Shall we send a wire?"

I reached for the phone. "We might lose a couple of

days that way," I said. "What's Sol Green's number?"

Sol's a publicity man who's well liked at NBC and specializes in handling Perry. When I gave him the pitch he said, "Sounds wonderful, Harry. Can I call you back?"

"I'll be here," I said.

He called back in twenty minutes. "Jeez," he said, "I forgot. That very night Perry is getting an award at the Astor. Red Cross or Community Chest or something."

I took Clare to lunch at "21." Figured it would give our morale a little boost. When we got back to the office there was a message to call Ed Sullivan's secretary. I think I had promised Ed an exclusive on our award story. You really have to break a thing like this open for everybody, but it doesn't do any harm now and then to let one of the boys get a lick at it a few hours early.

I told Ed's girl I had no news.

I was looking out the window at some pigeons that were trying to keep out of the rain when Clare said, "What about Jimmy Thomas?"

For a long time I looked at the pigeons, going over names in my mind. Groucho, Caesar, Berle, Gleason, Hope, Skelton, Silvers, Como. They were all off the list for one reason or another. Buttons, Cox, and a few others weren't working at the moment.

"Sugar plum," I said, "I think you have hit it. At least we'll give it a try."

Thomas was a new boy. Not as big yet as the old hands, but getting good ratings and a great press, which was important. To me, I mean. Personally, I didn't entirely dig his talent but I knew a lot of people who did. To me he seemed cast in Godfrey's mold, although he had a youthful, fresh appeal; but I knew a few people who thought he was the funniest thing since Charlie Chaplin.

"Where does Thomas hail from?" I said. "Cincinnati?"

"Chicago," Clare said.

"Good. We'll get good breaks there."

"You're chicken-counting," Clare said, and she was right. I didn't have Thomas' name on the dotted line yet.

I thought about him while I reached for the phone. Jimmy had started out down South as a disc jockey and had landed in Chicago after the war. His easygoing, country-boy charm and his way of handing out a line of gab between records had made him, within three years, the toast of the town, so CBS finally brought him to New York. But somebody goofed and they had him doing quiz shows for a couple of years, which made him a big favorite with the afternoon crowd but didn't make much of an impression at Lindy's. Finally, though, he had gotten a summer-replacement spot on a kind of last-minute fluke, and that did it. He was off to the races.

Funny thing about television. In the old days you worked for years to become a star. In TV one good show could do it. And, Jimmy did a good show; I'll have to admit that. He worked mostly ad-lib, although he had writers, and his peculiar combination of boy-next-door style and sharp wit made him the critics' darling. Not since Buttons and Gobel has anybody made it that fast. Within six weeks his name was as well known around the country as anybody in the business. It remained to be seen, of course, whether or not he could last, but for the time being he was certainly riding high.

I got his press agent on the line. "Andy," I said, playing it carefully, "I've just heard news that I thought you might be interested in."

"What's that?" he said.

"Been talking to the gang over here and they're very hot to give Jimmy the big one this year. You know, the Mr. Entertainment award. It's between him and Gleason, as it stands at the moment."

"Jeez," Andy said. "It would be a great thing for Jim. When are they voting? When will you know?"

Andy hasn't been in the business long. He used to write or something.

"Oh," I said, "maybe this afternoon, maybe not for a couple of days. Reason I'm calling you now is just to get a line on a few things. Like would Jimmy be available to accept the award on the twenty-seventh of April? In case he wins, I mean."

"Don't see why not," Andy said. "He never gets away and he has nothing booked in the way of benefits or anything, after—let me see—the middle of March."

"Well," I said, "I'll tell them that over here and we'll see what happens."

"Swell," Andy said. "Very nice of you to call, Harry."

I played it cool and killed a couple of hours to bring Andy and Thomas to a boil. Got some dictation done, went out and got a haircut, and then came back and began doing a little thinking as to the dais line-up for the banquet. I figured it would be the usual: somebody from the mayor's office; somebody speaking for the governor, a couple of columnists, whatever glamour dolls were scheduled to be in town to plug pictures; a couple of other comics or emcees from CBS, Thomas' network; three or four officers of the organization, and a toastmaster. Jessel had done it for us two years before, so we probably couldn't get him.

While I was jotting down some names Andy called back. It was twenty minutes past four.

"I've talked to Jim," he said, "and he's very pleased to be in the running. He would definitely be available on the twenty-seventh."

"Funny thing you should call at just this minute," I said. "I had the phone in my hand trying to call *you*. Good news."

"Really?"

"Yep. It was never even close. They love Gleason but Jimmy is hot this year."

"Gee, that's wonderful."

"You bet it is," I said, "but then Jim deserves it. I love his show myself."

"Thanks," Andy said. "I'll tell him."

"You should get the wire from the old man any minute," I said, signaling Clare to get it out on the other phone. "Then in a couple of days we'll fill you in with the minor details."

"Wonderful," Andy said. "I'll let you guys make the first announcement, then I'll follow it up. You let me know how you want to handle it."

"Oh, by the way," I said, "maybe Jim could work a couple of plugs for the organization into the show some time this week."

"No problem," Andy said. "Shoot it over and we'll put it on."

Frankly, I pride myself on never overlooking anything. Thomas does one of those chatty shows where you can

get plugs in easy. It's tougher if you're working with somebody like Hope or Berle.

Within a week we had the dais line-up all nailed down.
We were able to get Phil Silvers. Phil couldn't be on hand
for the whole thing but he committed himself to come in
for ten minutes and say a few words. Carmine De Sapio
signed on because he likes our organization and because I
suggested he could make a brief pitch about his candidate.
I like Carmine. He's the kind of a guy who'll usually come
through for you. Then we got Rhonda Fleming because
her picture was opening the same day as the banquet; Earl
Wilson because he prided himself on being the guy who
had "discovered" Thomas when he was working in Chicago; Jaye P. Morgan because she had been named the
Queen of our Winter Fund-Raising Drive and thought she
owed us something; Mike Wallace because he was still kind
of new to the banquet circuit, and was impressed at being
invited and wanted to be a nice guy about it; Herbert
Bayard Swope because he was on our Board of Trustees;
and two CBS vice-presidents because it was part of their
day's work. The other four chairs, as I say, were taken by
officers of the organization. They were all *part-time* officers, of course, as they had their own business to attend
to in addition to their charitable activities, but they were
all ready, willing, and able to attend because they got a
kick out of hobnobbing with the celebrities.

If I do say so myself everything went off smooth as
glass.

The Grand Ballroom of the Waldorf was darned near
filled up the night of the banquet and we had pretty lights
and a small band playing dinner music.

We hadn't had any luck getting a topnotch emcee, so we finally had to settle for Peter O'Brien from the Mayor's office, who is pretty good. He's kind of a minor-league Grover Whalen as far as I'm concerned, but he tells a fair story, the ladies like him, and he handles a banquet with all the ease of a man who has practically lived on chicken, peas, and ice cream.

The feed was pretty good, and about nine-forty-five I gave O'Brien the high sign and sent the man over to adjust the microphone. I felt fine. The pictures had already been taken, the money was all in, I had had a couple of drinks and, all in all, life was rosy.

While I was watching the guy adjust the mike I noticed that Andy Sloan, Thomas' man, was approaching my table. He hunched down next to me.

"Say," he said, "Jim was just wondering—who did the voting that got him this award?"

I've always thought it was pretty corny in stories where people say their blood ran cold, but, believe me, that's the way I felt right then. I personally always had figured Thomas as kind of a smart-aleck type and I was afraid that his question meant trouble.

"Why, what do you mean, Andy?" I stalled.

"You know, who decided that he's this year's Mr. Entertainment? Was there some kind of a vote? Jim just wants to know in connection with his speech."

I started to say, "That's what I was afraid of," but I held my tongue.

"Well," I said, "you know how these things work. There's no actual vote. It was just the committee. Same way we do it every year. Like for Groucho and the rest of them."

"Who's on the committee?"

"Well, uh—I mean it's not a *formal* committee or any-thing. We just discuss it up at the office and we do a lot of thinking as to who's the most deserving guy and like that."

"I see," Andy said. "Okay, thanks. I'll tell Jim."

I figured there was no sense running after him.

"What were you two whispering about?" Clare said.

"Listen," I said. "Wasn't it Thomas who made that speech about fluoridation on his show a few weeks ago?"

"Yes," she said. "Why do you ask?"

"I don't see the Thomas show too often. Does he think he's some sort of a—like a—you know, an Edward R. Murrow?"

"Yes, maybe a little. But what's up?"

"The jig. Sloan just came nosing around to find out how we actually do the deciding about the award."

"So?"

"So I told him."

"Why didn't you lie?"

"I don't know. What good would that have done? They could check later."

"Are you afraid Thomas is going to mention something about it in his speech?"

"Two minds," I said, "with but a single thought. The papers would eat it up. We'd be out of work in the morning."

Clare put her hand to her head and just stared at the tablecloth.

I looked across the room. Sloan and Thomas had their heads together, with Sloan doing the talking and Thomas frowning. After a moment he lifted his head and looked at me. I pretended not to notice and gawked at the giant chandelier for a couple of seconds. When I looked back, Thomas was still staring at me, with what the fiction boys would probably describe as a sardonic smile on his face.

At that moment O'Brien rapped for order, cleared his throat, and said, "Good evening, ladies and gentlemen. Can you hear me?"

A man at a nearby table shouted "Yes!"

"Not you, Charley." O'Brien laughed. "I said ladies and *gentlemen.*"

You had to hand it to Pete. He was fast on his feet.

After he handled a few formal introductions and announcements, Pete introduced Mr. Salzberger, our chairman, who lumbered to the microphone, spilled a glass of water, discussed finances briefly, and sat down.

Pete then told a few stories and got the crowd in a good mood. Me, I didn't laugh.

After that it was Carmine, whose remarks had something to do with the opportunities in our great nation for young men with something fresh and worth-while to say, although he had a little trouble working in praise for both Jimmy Thomas and his candidate. Then came Rhonda Fleming, who said she couldn't really think of very much to say because she wasn't a practiced public speaker but that to prove just how much she loved Jim, she was going to give him a big kiss right then and there, and she did, and the crowd ate it up. Thomas wasn't exactly displeased either. I mean, after all.

She closed with a few words about the organization and only said "worthy cause" twice, which is less than par for the course.

Then Earl said a few words, and I do mean a few words because he isn't much of a talker, which is true of a lot of writers, but he spoke sincerely anyway and did an okay job. Then O'Brien put Phil on because he had to get out early and he was great, of course, as always. We should have given him the award. He's not the type that asks questions.

"It's very wonderful to be here at the—" he said and then he looked at a small card in his hand and said, "the Waldorf." It broke everybody up because he was pretending not to know where he was, you know.

"I think it's a fine thing that you're giving this well-deserved citation to Jimmy Thomas," he said, "although frankly I think there is one other man to whom the award could have gone—myself."

Phil actually is a very shy, modest guy, you understand, but sometimes he does these jokes where he seems to be bold or brazen and the people eat it up. Anyway, he went on like that for about eight minutes and he even had Thomas laughing, which is pretty good because being the guest of honor at one of these affairs is a little unnerving and you are apt to be kind of distracted during the speeches and what-have-you. I was hoping Thomas would choke.

At long last we were heading for the home stretch and O'Brien picked up the large, shiny plaque we had had made up.

"As you all know," Peter said, "the Mr. Entertainment Award that this organization presents every year is one of the most respected in the annals of show business. Extreme care is given to the selection of candidates for this great honor, and when a man is privileged to have his name engraved on one of these plaques, it is a tremendously significant thing, both to the man involved, to the organization, and to . . . uh . . . those of us who support this worthy effort."

I looked at Clare and smiled to hide the fact that I felt sick.

"We all know," he was saying, "the tireless devotion and unflagging zeal with which show people contribute their time and talents to one charitable cause or another. It has been said that an actor is the only man in the world who will time and time again give away the only thing he has to sell: his God-given ability."

I didn't quite see what that had to do with Jimmy's getting the award, but the crowd seemed to be lapping it up and, besides, I suppose Thomas had done his share of benefits, although I must say he had never done anything in particular for our organization before. But be that as it may, O'Brien was warming to his task, as they say.

"This young man," he said, "who came out of the great city of Chicago just a few years ago, has done what very few men in our history have been able to do. He has won the heart of New York, the respect of its people, and the admiration of its leaders. New York is proud to consider Jimmy Thomas an adopted son."

At this there was a great wave of applause.

"And how has he accomplished all this?" O'Brien asked. "By consistently telecasting good, clean entertainment" (more applause), "by bringing a smile to many a troubled countenance, by giving unselfishly of his time and . . . uh . . .

talent . . . and . . . uh . . . by showing the world what is meant by good, clean American entertainment."

The audience applauded again. Clare and I exchanged glances.

"Jimmy Thomas," O'Brien said, plunging into a brief biography, "was the only child of Alfred and Agnes Thomas of Baltimore, Maryland. As a boy he attended school in Baltimore, became interested in dramatics, and finally started his radio career on a Baltimore station. His professional progress was interrupted by a three-year stretch in the United States Navy" (more applause) "after which he migrated to Chicago and began the phenomenal success story that has reached its climax, so to speak, here in this room tonight. But I am certain that, in another sense, this is not the climax of the career of Jimmy Thomas. For he is yet a young man. He has horizons before him. Uncharted seas to sail. Battles to win. And great honors to . . . uh . . . attain. No, it will be many a year before Jimmy Thomas reaches the climax, the apex, of his climb to fame and the full love of . . . uh . . . his fellow Americans. And we know he will . . . uh . . . do all that we . . . uh . . . so confidently predict for him here tonight. At this time, it gives me extreme pleasure, Jim, to present to you this plaque." Thomas rose to his feet and stood, somewhat sheepishly, next to O'Brien. "It gives me extreme pleasure to present to you this citation for meritorious entertainment service to the people of America during the past twelve months and to officially proclaim you, acting as I am on behalf of this great organization, Mr. Entertainment of 1956!"

The whole audience leaped to its feet and gave Thomas a lengthy ovation.

When it subsided he bowed, looked directly at me, and then spoke slowly. "Thank you, Mr. O'Brien, ladies and gentlemen, and distinguished guests. I know this has been a long evening for you and I'm not going to take very much of your time now with a speech or anything remotely resembling a speech. I just want to say a few words about this award . . . and about what it means."

I couldn't look at Clare.

"You know, those of us in the entertainment field receive quite a few awards. Our offices are full to overflowing with plaques and citations and gold cups and silver cups and what-have-you. Not all of these awards, frankly, are of earth-shattering importance. Some are presented not so much for the honor of the recipient as for the publicizing of the donor."

I looked at the Old Man, wondering if he had sized up the situation, but his face was a mask as he sat turned slightly sideways, staring at Thomas.

"But I want to make it clear," our award winner went on, "that I am truly grateful . . . to all of you . . . for the kind words said here tonight . . . and for this very handsome plaque. I know what your organization stands for . . . and what its ideals are. And I like thinking that those ideals are somehow embodied in, or connected with, this particular award."

I looked at Clare. She looked kind of funny. Like she almost had tears in her eyes or something.

"Those of us in television," Jimmy said, "sometimes are apt to get so interested in the very *doing* of our programs that we almost forget the audience, strange as that may sound. It isn't that we're unaware of the audience; it's just that the simple mechanics of our work sometimes induces in us a peculiar kind of . . . well, you might call it . . . selfishness. And that's why it's particularly heart-warming to receive some demonstration such as this of the fact that you don't hold that selfishness against us, that you do have some measure of charitable feeling toward us, and that you look to us to bring some pleasure into your lives.

"Despite what you may hear, we *are* interested in you, of course. Sometimes I wish I could go into your homes physically and do my program. At times I feel that the camera stands in the way of our getting to know each other, and it is, as I say, an evening like this and an event like this, that does bring me face to face with you and that enables me to thank you very sincerely and very humbly for your response and your affection. I"—he paused and scratched his head with that peculiar country-boy gesture that made him seem so folksy—"I guess I just finished my speech, folks, so . . . so I think I'll just sit down. Thank you again, from the bottom of my heart."

The crowd gave Thomas a swell hand and I was a little surprised when I noticed who was applauding the loudest. It was me. To this day I still haven't made up my mind how much of a smart aleck Thomas is, but I have to admit he had the good sense to realize that the last thing the people want is a cold, hard fact shoved down their throats.

That's about all there is to this little saga. When you started reading it you probably figured me for a cynical bastard who just wanted to give you the low-down on the citation business, but that isn't my angle. I mean, as we all left the Waldorf that night Jimmy Thomas was happy, the audience was happy, the treasury was bulging, and Clare and I were set for another year. Don't give me any of that ends-and-means malarky. I like my work very much. Wouldn't change it for anything.

Oh, and one more thing. This year when you're taking care of the Community Chest and the Red Cross and the March of Dimes and the rest, remember the organization, too, will you?

8

The Saint

MARTIN lay on his stomach, feeling the unyielding rock pressing flatly against his ribs. The desert sun had baked the dull stone during the morning and now, late in the day, the stored-up warmth, relaxing the tension of his muscles, almost tempted him to sleep.

His beard matted damply under his jaw; through it his interlocked hands supported his chin. Squinting against the reflected light slanting up off the desert floor, he looked down at the road that passed along a small defile beneath his position, waiting. It had been over an hour since anyone had passed along the trail and he was becoming impatient for the sight of another human. Squirming with some pain up into a kneeling position, he threw his head back and stared fiercely at the sky. Then he smiled and said as loudly as he could, "Oh, Almighty God, please deign to send someone along the road, for I am desolate in my—in my——" For a moment Martin considered how he might gracefully end his prayer, but at last, feeling himself unequal to the task, he broke off and prayed for a few minutes silently. The prayers that were thought rather than spoken were easier to handle. He could not stutter within the privacy of his mind and if a word failed him, if an idea was developed obscurely, the realization never was crystallized so that he had the impression that his unspoken thoughts had a great dignity and symmetry that his more formal vocal entreaties could not equal.

Rising stiffly, he walked to the overhanging rock that had been his roof for the past fortnight and there, in a sliver of shade, began to eat the few dates he had left. The sugar in them was immediately sucked off into his weakened system and revived him somewhat, but at the same time it gave him a terrible thirst with the result that he had to climb down the hill to the road and then walk half a mile to the nearest well to refresh himself. Twice along the way he toyed with the idea of giving up his hermit's existence, but each time the possibility occurred to him he regarded it as a temptation of Satan and prayed vigorously for strength, which, it seemed, was thereupon vouchsafed.

At the well he publicly offered his blessing to two women who were filling goatskin bags. They regarded him silently as he called down upon them the beneficence of heaven and then, having completed their work, nudged a small donkey and departed without saying a word to him.

After he had drunk his fill he hurried back off down the road, walking swiftly so as to catch up with the women. After a few minutes he came within sight of them and called loudly, "Do not worry about your water jugs, for it has been said, 'Take no thought for your life, what ye

shall eat or what ye shall drink, nor yet for your body
what ye shall put on.'"

The women turned, glanced back fearfully, and increased
their pace somewhat.

"Behold the fowls of the air," Martin shouted, "they sow
not, neither do they reap, nor gather into barns, yet your
heavenly Father feeds them."

One of the women turned without slackening her speed
and said, "Peace, brother."

"I did not come to bring peace," Martin shouted, "but a
sword; and to set brother against brother and daughter
against daughter and father against mother."

The women walked on in the hot sunlight, Martin following them at several paces.

"I have given up all that I owned," Martin said.

"Good for you," said the taller of the two women.

"A rich man cannot enter the Kingdom of Heaven,"
Martin said.

"So we have heard," the woman returned.

"Resist thee not evil," Martin said, speaking somewhat
more softly, "but whosoever shall smite thee on thy right
cheek, turn to him the other also."

The women did not answer.

"Let your light so shine before men that they may see
your good works and glorify your Father, who is in
heaven," he intoned.

The donkey whinnied softly and ambled slowly on
through the dust.

After a few minutes Martin stopped in his tracks and
raised his voice to its former volume. "Do you not intend
to heed what I am saying?" he cried.

"We are busy," said the tall woman, "and we must return to our homes and families."

"Woe be unto you," Martin shouted, stamping his foot. "Woe be unto you because—because—" but he could think of no words of his own to express the contempt that welled within his heart; he could create no phrases to match the sentiments that seethed inside him. "An eye for an eye and a tooth for a tooth," he screamed at last, at the disappearing figures. "The angels will—will descend and cast you into the fire—and there shall be weeping and gnashing of teeth."

Tears began to stream from Martin's eyes as the mixed feelings of impotent rage and love for God boiled in his breast.

"My God, my God," he cried, "why hast Thou forsaken me?"

A hawk circled silently high overhead, gliding on boiling air. When Martin at length began to walk again, this time off to his hermit's retreat, it veered away and disappeared.

When he had climbed back up to his flat rock he could perceive, at a great distance, the figures of the two women and their beast.

"Witches," he cried after them, and the desert rocks echoed his voice, "thou shalt not suffer a witch to live!"

Picking up a stone, he threw it after them, futilely. "And thou shalt stone him with stones that he die," he said. At last, tiring, he lay down full length on the warm rock and cradled his head sideways on his folded arms that he might rest but still be able to survey the road. He thought about the women for several minutes and eventually came to concentrate on the tall one, who had had lustrous, dark eyes, and a full mouth. He saw her as the personification of evil and wished that he might encounter her again, at the well or anywhere, in order that he might denounce her publicly or, better yet, strike her with his fist in the name of the Lord, punish her physically for what he imagined must be her many and colorfully varied sins.

He would beat her to her knees, he considered, and then, while she pleaded for mercy, rip her sinful garments from her body that her shame might be exposed to the merciless eye of the sky. Squinting slightly, looking sideways now, he could almost see her lying in the dust of the road below, her clothing in disarray, her bosom heaving in remorse and fear, her eyes turned toward him in supplication. He could almost see her lifting her hands to him, catching hold of his robes, pitifully pulling herself close to his body, pressing her detestable warmth against him.

It was then that Martin gave a great shout and, rising, began to pull off his own garments. In a moment he stood naked under the blazing sun, stomping up and down and crying wordlessly to the heavens. In this state, he considered, he might romp in the pure innocence of Eden, undefiled by the skin of lustful beasts, unhampered in his sheer pulsing desire to be at one with nature and the hum and slide of the universe. Looking afar, he could no longer clearly see the women although he could still faintly make out that something moved along the trail in the distance, raising a pale puff of smoky dust. Suddenly he was consumed with a wish to see them again and, leaping from boulder to ledge to slant of ground, he clambered down to the trail and began to run after the women. "They toil not," he screamed, "neither do they spin, and yet Solomon in all his glory was not arrayed——"

At that moment Martin came to a full stop and over his

browned face there came an expression of horror. His eyes glared fiercely at the horizon and then at the sky and then down at his wiry body, and at that moment he began to writhe as well as to claw at the flesh of his stomach and thighs with his fingernails. His mind a tornado of lust and sensitivity to the blueness of the sky, the warmth of the sun on his body, the lazy grace of a passing vulture, the soft lavender of the distant mountains, he sobbed half-words of prayer and tender carnal sentiment.

After a while a smile came over his features, although his eyes were still wet with tears, for he knew now for the first time in a long time what he had to do. There were the long, seemingly endless hours and days of fasting and prayer and doubt and then there came the blinding moments of certainty and strength. This was one of them. Turning away from the women, he ran back toward his home among the rocks, toward his meager cache of belongings, his walking stick, his water bag, his extra sandals, his outer cloak, and his knife.

"Oh, yes," he cried, "it has been made clear to me. The Scripture tells me plainly." He laughed triumphantly as his body slithered whitely up the low hill. Once, as he fell, broken desert rocks scraped his pale skin cruelly. He suffered the pain with a feeling of glory and threw himself headlong again that he might again be tortured. A worthy sentiment, he considered, but it was only delaying the supreme act, the culmination of all his years of prayer and trial.

He had sinned, clearly and beyond question of doubt, in thinking of the woman. His mind has been delirious with pleasure at the idea of her nearness and his body had contorted and wrestled with itself in a frenzy of guilt and excitement. There remained nothing now but to complete the act, to solve the problem, expiate his sin, drop the curtain on his drama.

Another moment and he knelt trembling, reaching into the shadow of the stone that protected his few belongings. The knife was partly rusty and its sharpness left something to be desired, but it would serve. It would have to. Destiny could not be delayed.

"If thy right hand offend thee," Martin shouted to the silent desert, "cut it off!"

At that he knelt and placed his right forearm against a round stone. Thanking heaven that he was left-handed and could bring his entire strength therefore to bear, he jabbed the point into his right wrist and then brought the blade flat against the arm and pressed down as firmly as he could, shouting the while to distract his concentration from the pain. Surprisingly, there was very little. The job was done more readily than he had expected and when at last he had fulfilled the letter of the law he stood naked, staring up into the blank, terrible, cloudless blue of the universe, blood pouring from the end of his arm, turning his head from side to side, looking up the way a child might stand in its crib after a fright in the dark, looking longingly for a parent to enter, to pick it up, to comfort it and offer it the love that comes from strength.

9

The Blood of the Lamb

S LATER had been dozing, with his seat
belt still buckled around him, for perhaps ten minutes when
he felt someone tapping his elbow.

It was the man next to him in the aisle seat, the small,
wispy-looking man with the gold-rimmed glasses.

"I beg your pardon, sir," the man said, smiling. "I
thought perhaps you might enjoy having some reading matter." Slater looked down and saw that he was holding out
a pamphlet.

"Thanks," he said. "Thanks a lot." The pamphlet had
a white cover on which was printed *The Blood of the
Lamb*. When Slater saw that it was a religious tract, he
experienced a slight flicker of embarrassment without being able to understand the reason for the feeling. For a
moment he sat half-turned toward the man, expecting a
continuation of the conversation, but the stranger had taken

a pencil from his inside coat pocket and was busily occupied in making a notation on a small piece of paper.

Slater looked at his watch and then out the window.
Flat-bottomed clouds were shelved with seeming firmness
about three thousand feet below the plane; above, all was
blue infinity washed in sunshine. At that moment one of
the stewardesses passed along the aisle carrying a paper cup
full of water, and automatically Slater turned, admiring
the trim fit of her gabardine skirt. When his head had
ninety-degreed to the left he suddenly became aware that
the stranger was looking at him. Clearing his throat, he
reluctantly opened the pamphlet.

The heading on the first page was "An Open Letter to
Men of Good Will." As he read, Slater became conscious
of the little man's breathing and then, by pretending to
check the air vent overhead, he glanced to the side without
turning his head and saw that the man's eyes were fixed
on the open page.

"Since men of science and men of politics," the pamphlet said, "have created a physical detonation and an
A-bomb-ination unto the Lord, we offer as a panacea for
the ills of the world the news of an H-bomb: a Heaven-
bomb. Not very long ago it became abundantly clear to
those with eyes to see and ears to hear that Satan was on
the loose and sat in the palaces of the world. However, it
has been written 'the Devil is mighty but God is almighty,'
so those of us who have been or are willing to be or are
not opposed to being washed in the Blood of the Lamb
have faith that we will be lifted up and made safe even in
the midst of the coming holocaust."

"Amen," the stranger whispered softly in Slater's ear.

Slater said, "Oh, God," moving his lips but making no

sound. Only twenty minutes out of New York, almost three hours before the plane was scheduled to land at Chicago and here he was, trapped by a religious fanatic.

Having nowhere else to turn, he returned to the pamphlet.

" 'The wrath of men worketh not the righteousness of God (Jas. 1:20),' " he read. " 'Be not afraid of them that kill the body (Luke 12:4) . . . .' but desire only to drinketh of the Blood of the Lamb and ye shall be saved. For I say unto you that whosoever shall make an a-bomb-ination in the sight of the most High shall not avail himself of the graces of the Lord's at-one-ment (atonement)!"

Slater closed the booklet and pinched the bridge of his nose.

"What's the matter, brother?" the little man said.

"What?" Slater said, a nervous itch spreading across his chest.

"Aren't you receptive to the message of the Lord?"

"Yes," Slater said, "it's just that I—I'm somewhat tired and the print is a bit small for my eyes."

"Better stick with it, brother," the man said, "there isn't much time."

"Much time for what?" Slater asked, feeling a vague uneasiness above and beyond the simple embarrassment the conversation was calculated to arouse in him.

"In the world ye shall have tribulation," the man said. "John, sixteen, thirty-three."

"Yes," Slater agreed lamely, "I guess you shall."

"So?" the man said.

"So what?" Slater said.

"Oh, Lord, be merciful," the man said, looking to the ceiling. "Brother, I am trying to give you a friendly, fair warning. Prepare your soul."

Impatient, Slater considered pretending to want to go to the lavatory and then seeing if he could change his seat. But looking back and forward through the plane's length, he could see that all the seats were occupied. It was the damned holiday traffic, he recalled; he'd even had difficulty getting accommodations on the flight at all. Gritting his teeth, he said, "Prepare my soul for what?"

"For the crash," the man said, smiling fiercely.

For several seconds Slater stared at the pamphlet, then out the window, then at the hostess flashing her teeth between red lips at the front of the plane. His mind was filled with impressions, half-thoughts, and halting plans, but for some reason he could not find voice. At length he cleared his throat.

"Did you hear me, brother?" the man said. "I'm giving you the word of the Lord out of the goodness of my heart."

Slater started to say, "Thank you," and then silently cursed himself.

"There is not a just man upon the earth, that doeth good and sinneth not," the man said, "Ecclesiastes seven, twenty."

"I suppose that's right," Slater said. "Frankly I'm not as familiar with the Bible as I might be."

"Who is?" the man said, genially enough. "That's why I've been sent to do the work of the Lord and spread the glad tidings of the Heaven-bomb."

"What bomb is that?" Slater asked.

"Fear not," the man said. "The trumpet shall sound and the dead shall be raised. But I'm pleased to hear, my friend, that you are interested. I spoke to some of the other passengers in the waiting room and they ignored me. But soon," he said, and his lip curled with a ferocious sneer, "their blood will wash the expression of contempt from their sinful faces."

"What do you mean by that?" Slater persisted, feeling compelled to make sense out of the man's message, wanting to clear up the aura of threat that hung over his words.

At that moment the other stewardess loomed above them with a clip-board and a pencil. "Name, please," she said, smiling at Slater. "Henry Slater," he said, wanting to speak to her about the man but not knowing how to start.

"Your name, sir?" she said to the stranger.

"Percy Warren," the man said, "Tulsa, Oklahoma. Would you care to have some interesting reading material, young lady?"

"Why, yes, thank you," the girl said, opening her eyes wide as if speaking to a child. "Thank you so much." She took the tract and tucked it into the pocket of her jacket. Slater was surprised to see Warren reach a speckled, blue-veined hand into her pocket and extract the pamphlet. "Here," he said, "you'd better read that pretty quick, while there's still time."

The girl's mouth opened blankly and then she said, "Certainly, sir, just as soon as I've finished here." She looked at Slater with a slight smile as if to ask if his companion were making a joke, and Slater took advantage of her concentration to frown and carefully touch his right forefinger to his temple in a sort of smooth movement with a follow-through so that the man would not notice.

The girl evidently got the idea of his message. "Let's see," she said, "you're getting off at Chicago; is that right, Mr. Warren?"

"The dead, small and great, shall stand before God,"

Warren said, "and they shall be judged according to their works."

The girl smiled automatically, turned with no apparent haste, and walked slowly forward to the pilot's cabin.

For perhaps a minute nothing happened. The monotonous drone of the plane's motors began to induce in Slater an almost hypnotic calm. Perhaps, he thought, the whirring in Warren's head had run down. Perhaps he would not speak again. Another half-minute passed. It was like the sensation, familiar to parents, of waiting for a peevish baby to fall asleep, each passing uneventful second seeming to be a tiny triumph.

Suddenly the man leaped to his feet and began passing out pamphlets to people up and down the aisle. "And the dead shall be judged out of those things which were written in the books, according to their works," he shouted, his face wreathed in an unaccountable smile. At the far end of the plane somebody laughed and, closer, a woman gasped in fear.

Slater, now released by the man's movement, leaped to his feet and stepped into the aisle. Momentarily he considered taking the man, whose back was to him, by surprise, striking him a Judo blow on the back of the neck, the way he had learned in the Marines. But it would be ridiculous. Warren had made no threatening gestures. To attack him would be unjust. A man on the other side of the aisle tapped Slater's arm.

"He with you?" the man said.

"No," Slater said.

"What's the matter with him?"

"Damned if I know," Slater whispered. "He's nuts."

"Isn't somebody going to do something?" a woman behind them said.

"What do you suggest, lady?" Slater said.

"I don't know," the woman said, huddling back against her window as if to get out of harm's way.

At that moment the two stewardesses bore down upon Warren from the front of the plane.

"Mr. Warren," Slater heard one of them say, "I'd like very much to hear more about your—about your booklet. Did you write it?"

"I am a witness unto the Lord," Warren said loudly. "The Lord is the hand. I am the pencil."

"That sounds very interesting," the other girl said. "Why don't we go back to the lounge and talk about it?"

"Just a moment," Warren said. "I've got to give all these people the message and the warning."

"All right," said the first girl. "Listen, why don't I just give you a hand? Here, I can pass some of these out to the people up front."

"Why, that would be fine," Warren said, taking a short stack of booklets from his pocket. "You people up there pay attention to the young lady, you hear?"

"They hear," the girl said. "Or if they don't, I'll tell them."

The man across the aisle spoke out of the side of his mouth. "You've got to hand it to those girls," he said. "I wouldn't have known *what* to do with the bastard."

"Yeah," Slater said, in complete agreement. But there was still the matter of the warning. A warning against what?

"Here, Marge," the first girl said to her companion, "why don't you help by handing these out back that way?"

The second girl nodded, took half of the tracts Warren had given her companion, and moved to the rear of the plane, smiling at the passengers who looked up at her, lifting her eyebrows in a gesture of amused understanding as if Warren were only a naughty, exasperating child.

"Hurry up back there," Warren said, still standing in the aisle, toward the front of the plane. "Now, when you've all received your books, please open them to page fourteen. For there it is written: 'For if the dead rise not, then is not Christ raised.' First Corinthians, chapter fifteen, verse sixteen."

"Ah, shut up and sit down," somebody shouted from behind Warren.

He whirled as if stabbed in the back.

"What?" he screamed. "Do you refuse to hear the word of God?"

"My God," a woman said, near Slater. "Why did they do that? Why did they have to open their mouths up there?"

Somebody made a shushing noise and all eyes focused on Warren.

"Prepare to meet thy doom," he shouted. "You're all so smug and so self-satisfied, aren't you, you whited sepulchers?" He pronounced the word "suplukers." "Well, perhaps your hard hearts will be softened and turned toward the Lord when I tell you that this plane will never land!"

A woman screamed softly and a man's voice said, "Be quiet. Listen."

"That's right," Warren said, laughing. "*Now* there's nobody telling me to shut up, is there? Oh, no. *Now* things are a little different, aren't they? Well, it's too late now to come crawling to me, but, praise God, it's not too late to be washed in *the Blood of the Lamb*."

Behind Warren the co-pilot appeared, walking fast. "What's wrong here?" he said, his face frozen in an insincere smile.

"Wrong?" Warren screamed. "Nothing is wrong, my friend, except in the hearts of this assemblage that are blackened with sin."

"Hadn't you better sit down, sir?" the officer said.

"Certainly," Warren said, surprisingly. "It doesn't matter whether I stand or sit or what I do. What *is* important is that you all get it through your thick, sinful skulls that this plane will never land safely."

The co-pilot spun him around and snapped, "What do you mean by that?"

"Why," Warren said, "it's simplicity itself. You know what the plane is, don't you? And you know what to land means, don't you? And you know what safely means, don't you? Well, let's hope you understand just as clearly what it means to crash in flames of wrath!"

"Why do you say we're going to crash?" the officer demanded, making a pointless effort to lower his voice, to keep the passengers from hearing.

"Because, you idiots," Warren shouted, "there's a time bomb in my suitcase."

The co-pilot raced to the empty seat and grabbed Slater. "Where was he sitting?" he said.

"Right here," Slater said, stepping to one side.

Together they looked under the seat and in the rack overhead. They found nothing except a cheap straw hat.

"Christ, I thought maybe he had a small bag," the co-pilot said, racing back to Warren, grabbing him by the shoulders. "Listen, you, I'm going to ask you just once. Is your suitcase in the baggage compartment?"

"Where else would it be, you tool of Satan?" Warren shouted, smiling triumphantly.

"You men keep your eye on this bird," the co-pilot said, heading for the cockpit. "We're going back."

"You'll never make it," Warren chuckled.

Slater noticed that a woman near Warren had taken out a rosary and was praying half audibly, her lips moving. Warren spied her and cackled, "Six-sixty-six!"

"Should we rush him?" a baldheaded man said.

"What the hell good would that do?" Slater said. "We're in no danger from him; it's the damned bomb."

"Just remain in your seats," one of the stewardesses said, moving along the aisle. "The captain is radioing for instructions and landing clearance. We'll get back down as fast as we can."

At that moment the plane went into a steep bank and Warren stumbled, falling onto the lap of an elderly woman who screamed and shoved him back to a standing position.

"Would you please sit down, sir?" one of the hostesses said to Warren. "You might get hurt like this."

"That's a great one," the baldheaded man said.

"The wages of sin is death," Warren shouted. "Don't waste your time being angry at me, dear friends. I pray you, make good use of the last few remaining minutes to make your peace with God. Why is it that the world always reviles those of us who bring the glad tidings? They killed my Christ and ye would kill me, would you not, if your hands were not at this moment paralyzed with fear."

The baldheaded man ripped out an oath and ran forward at Warren, striking him a blow in the face. Warren fell

backward and rolled along the aisle as the plane suddenly
lost altitude in a sickening, slanting drop. The hostesses
restrained the baldheaded man and Warren got to his feet.
"That's it," he said, smiling. "That's what your vaunted
civilization has brought you after all these thousands of
years. Well, it's all right. Revile me. Spit upon me. Kill
me if you will; but if you do, remember you die shortly
thereafter yourself with murder on your soul. The Lord
has a special love for martyrs, for their blood mingles with
his own. Oh, praise God and drink the Blood of the Lamb."

The baldheaded man, breathing heavily, went back to
his seat, white-faced.

"Ladies and gentlemen," the voice of the captain said
over the loud-speaker, "please remain calm. We're going to
try to land soon, perhaps at Philadelphia. Fasten your seat
belts, please. We'll do our best."

"What the hell good are seat belts at a time like this?"
somebody said.

The co-pilot, his tanned face seeming paler now, came
down the aisle again and walked up close to Warren.

"This bomb," he said, half-whispering, "when do you
have it—— I mean, when do you think it's supposed to
go off?"

"That's for me to know and you to find out," Warren
said smugly.

"Listen, man," the co-pilot said, bringing his face close
to Warren's. "I don't want any trouble with you. I mean
personally. I happen to be a Christian. My grandfather
was a Baptist minister and my father was a simple, God-
fearing farmer. As one Christian to another, I'm asking
you—what time is that bomb set for?'"

For once Warren was silent.

The passengers passed the word back, telling about the co-pilot's clever approach. His calm self-control helped to reduce slightly the feeling of hysteria that had been about to take over the ship.

After a long pause the officer again said, "Tell me, sir, at once."

"All right," Warren said, looking at his watch. "I'm usually a little slow. What time is it now?"

"It's exactly two-forty-six," the co-pilot said.

"Then," said Warren, "that bomb is going to go off in fourteen minutes."

The officer pushed past him and raced to the front of the plane with the information.

Unfortunately Warren's announcement had been over-heard and within seconds everyone aboard had learned that the deadline was three o'clock. Somebody tearfully asked if Daylight Saving Time had any connection with the matter, and for a brief moment hope flickered up and down the cabin like an almost visible force, only to be dashed out when Warren pointed to his wrist watch and said, "Repent ye. Death shall be your lot in thirteen minutes."

For the first time Slater became aware that there were no children aboard. Unable to force himself to comply with the order to fasten seat belts, he sat cross-legged on the arm of Warren's still vacant seat, his feet in the aisle. Two women were crying but most of the passengers seemed stunned into silence.

Looking at them, Slater found his heart torn in two directions. Part of him was filled with anger. He wanted, like the baldheaded man, to strike out, to avenge. The other part tried to concentrate on the fact, the idea, of death. Strangely, a feeling of unreality softened what might otherwise have been his terror. He thought of Ellen and the children, picturing them as they must be at this moment, the children in school, the wife shopping or doing something with a vacuum cleaner or a paring knife. Then he thought of them receiving the news of his death and at that picture he winced and actually turned his head away, as if by so doing he could blot out the prospect.

In a moment he found his thoughts taking a religious turn, but then he considered Warren's motivation and found himself unable to concentrate upon his personal identity as a man and a creature of God. There was the inclination but it was immediately followed by the reaction, the feeling that in doing what Warren had demanded, in praying, in abasing himself, he was participating in a bargain with a madman. He spent several minutes in this confused state, his thoughts at last broken by the captain's voice on the intercom.

"Folks, we're down to under two thousand feet and we may make an emergency landing. Again may I remind you to fasten your seat belts securely and to remain calm. I'll do all I can to—to see that—that we get down all right."

Slater sat down now and fastened his belt. The only person standing was Warren who swayed in the aisle near the front of the plane, muttering to himself.

A man at the rear said, "What time is it?" and when another voice said, "Two-fifty-one," a woman shrieked and began to sob.

Slater found himself staring at his watch, so that he eventually had to make a firm, definite effort to pull his eyes away from the seemingly speeding minute hand.

Looking out the window, he could see that they were quite low now. Trees, houses, and a few automobiles were plainly visible.

"Folks," the pilot's voice droned, "we're going to try to land at a private field just about five minutes away. We're going in very slowly and as soon as we touch down I'm going to have to reverse the props because the field is not the right length for a plane this size. It may be a lit-tle—a little rough . . . so I repeat, fasten your seat belts tightly and remain calm. There's nothing else you can do. If everything goes—when we stop we'll have to move fast. We'll open the escape hatch and we'll open the regular passenger door and you'll all have to jump for it. There'll be no passenger-loading ramp, but it's not too much of a jump and we'll give you a hand. Please leave the plane calmly and without pushing and shoving. Miss Ryan and Miss Simonetti will give you instructions at the proper moment. It is now two-fifty-three."

"Make your peace with the Lord, my friends," Warren cried benignly. "Thou shalt worship the Lord, thy God, and Him only shalt thou serve."

Every eye on the plane was turned toward him with hatred, but he seemed not to notice.

Below, the land looked frighteningly hilly to Slater, but the calm voice of the pilot had brought him a degree of extra courage. He checked his watch. Six minutes before the bomb was timed to explode.

The plane shuddered as the flaps extended to their fullest width and the pilot reduced speed, dropping another hundred feet almost too quickly.

"Which of you," Warren sang, "if you had your lives

to live over again, now would not be a more willing servant unto the Lord, thy God? Which of you would not now gladly bargain to bathe daily in the Blood of the Lamb?"

When his watch said five minutes to three Slater conferred with the man across the aisle. "What time do you have?" he said.

"Four minutes to go by me," the man said. "I may be a few seconds fast."

Slater did not answer.

It seemed that two seconds later somebody said, "Three minutes to go." Unaccountably Slater found himself remembering the old jocular explanation of relativity, the line about kissing your girl for one minute seeming like no time at all but sitting on a hot stove for one minute seeming like eternity.

The plane lurched and stumbled lower in the sea of air, approaching bottom. Slater's fists were clenched, his palms wet.

"We're almost in, folks," the pilot announced. "We have no direct radio control with this field, but I believe they know we're coming in. I have—" he broke off.

"What's wrong?" a man said.

Nobody answered.

At that moment the plane shuddered sickeningly and lifted as the motors were gunned with a powerful roar. "There was a small plane landing on the runway," the pilot said, his voice sounding uneven. "We're going to have to go around and make another pass at it."

"My God," the baldheaded man said, "we'll never make it. This plane will have to make such a big turn we can't possibly get down before three o'clock."

Thirty seconds before three o'clock Slater found himself tightening into a knot, blinking his eyes as if waiting for a door to slam, for his face to be slapped, for a gun to go off, or a life to end.

The plane leaned far to the left as the pilot fought for altitude to make the second pass. The treetops looked remarkably close to the lower wing-tip.

"Holy God," Warren said, "we praise Thy name."

By Slater's watch there were fifteen seconds left. Ten. He braced himself, placing the soles of his shoes against the seat in front of him. Even if they blew up, perhaps at this low altitude they might skid in. He counted off seven seconds to himself and sat rigidly, squinting, feeling cowardly, his chest wriggling with fear.

"It's after three," somebody shouted.

The baldheaded man shouted at Warren, "You son-of-a-bitch," he said, "that thing was supposed to go off just now. Well, is it or isn't it?"

"Let every soul be subject unto the higher powers," Warren said meekly, looking faint.

The plane had gotten turned around and now was lumbering clumsily out of the sky. The landing was bad and jolting and when the props were reversed there was a sickening lurch forward, as if the tail was going to go up in the air. It lifted noticeably and bumped down again hard and then at last they knew they were not going to crash.

Warren had fallen to the floor and now he was on his feet, but so was everyone else, despite the captain's plea for calm. They all jostled forward and when the co-pilot had opened the door they began piling out, the first to hit the ground turning to break the fall of the others. One man who had gotten out started to run from the plane but somebody said, "Come on back, you bastard, and help these women down."

Within two minutes they were all out and away from the plane except Warren, who stood forlornly inside the door, looking out and up at the sky.

"Come down out of there," the pilot shouted. "You'll be killed."

"No, I won't," Warren said, his hair lifting in the wind that whipped across the field. In the distance they heard the wail of a siren and now from both sides of the landing strip people began to approach.

"Keep back there," the pilot shouted. "There's a bomb on that plane that may go off any second. Keep back."

"What does he want to do," somebody said, pointing at Warren, "kill himself?"

Half an hour later two policemen put a ladder up to the side of the plane and dragged Warren out. At the local station, while they were telephoning for bomb-disposal information, he said, "You needn't bother. There's no bomb in my suitcase."

"What?" the man on the phone said, interrupting his call.

"I said there's nothing to worry about," Warren answered. "I just wanted to prove to those people how terrible it is that our generation has forgotten God. We have made an a-bomb-ination in His sight. Somebody had to bring us to our senses and announce the news of the H-bomb. The Heaven-bomb."

"All right, Pop," the policeman said. "You get in this

cell back here and lie down. I think we'd better keep you away from the other passengers."

"Give them my love," Warren said. "Tell them we all are saved by the Blood of the Lamb."

10

The Purpose and the Name

I HEREBY proclaim a new religion.

At the heart of it is the belief that there is no purpose to the existence of the world. Since God is all and the essence of perfection, He did not need to create us.

Rumble a roll softly on the big drum, brother.

Why we are here then has never and can never be agreed upon. The question suggests itself: If we do not know why we are here, are we even certain that we *are* here?

You have heard it said: "I think, therefore I am." I tell you rather that this is as close as we can come to truth: I think I am, therefore I think I am.

How I could use a good eclipse of the moon right now! I haven't had one in what seems like ages.

It is better to light one little candle, even if the candle is set delicately into the fuse mechanism of a bomb.

We will wear an emblem the true significance of which will be a subject of controversy. Controversy leads to bloodshed. Red is the brightest color. Perhaps there would be fewer murders if blood were colored a pale violet.

Love your enemies while they are still your friends.

Every monstrous criminal was once a warm, smiling cuddlesome baby.

Your leaders cannot feel humility for themselves. You must feel it for them. The best way is to think of the most powerful men one by one, in the order of their glory, picturing each of them in turn going to the toilet. It is *not* a disgusting thought, madam. After all, you must admit that it leads inevitably to the idea of the brotherhood of man. Can an evil tree bear good fruit?

Don't answer that.

"Now just a moment," a tall, stern-faced man at the back of the crowd said. "I have heard about enough."

Then plug up your ears, brother. Or walk away. But that won't really do the trick, will it? For what you really want is not simply to hear no more of me. You truly want to injure me because you do not approve of what I am saying, isn't that it?

Behold the lights of Times Square—the many-colored lights, winking and popping. Behold the swarming, smirking people, each an island of self-interest. Behold the taxi cabs and the chauffeured limousines and the cars with the out-of-town license plates. You must admit, brother, that this is a far more suitable place to serve as a letter-drop from the Almighty than a deserted hilltop. Here we have no lack of witnesses. Close your great big three-D full-color eyes for a moment and just open your stereophonic hi-fi ears. Let the waves of sound wash into your brain. There's a broken heart for every sound on Broadway.

What, brother? God is all? Don't step back off the curb, brother. You'll step on Him.

Don't tell me I blaspheme, dear friend. It's *you* who are guilty of this fearful sin. I was simply trying to demonstrate where your philosophy must inevitably lead. But don't worry. It's a trick you can do with anyone's philosophy.

Two policemen sauntered by, looking at the small crowd with faces that were blank except for an almost invisible, wearily exasperated compression of the lips at the corners of the mouth.

"Here we go gathering nuts in May," said one policeman to the other.

Anybody here played with a poisonous serpent or drunk cyanide or moved any mountains or spoken in divers tongues lately?

But don't worry, dear friends; I just said that to pull you into the store, as it were. The important thing I have to tell you tonight concerns the earth on which we stand. You don't know it's real name, do you?

What's that? The Earth?

No, my friends. The word "earth" is a common noun, not a proper one. Try as you may to imply a capital letter by your tone of voice, the fact remains that while we may have given the other planets names (and who gave us the right, by the way?), we do not know the name of our own. That is, *you* do not know the name of the earth. But I do. And I will tell you, dear friends.

After which I will pass among you to allow you to express your appreciation by killing me.

Let me go into a little background. There have been sixteen crucified saviors, dear brethren. Please understand I know that the one we revere is the supreme and the true—I am simply telling you the facts of history. Which is by way of respectfully pointing out the similarity of all men's essential religious beliefs and aspirations. I speak unity, dear friends, not dissension. But, as you shall learn, I also speak resignation and despair.

A light rain began to fall over the city and the black pavement of Times Square glistened and shone with a million twisted rainbows of light. Straight lines and bars of color high overhead were translated into wiggled streaks and blobs on the oily-pitch street. People began to compete for taxis.

The crowd huddled closer, although around the edges of the group a few individuals turned up their collars and drifted away into the night.

It has been found that certain symbols and dreams are universal. It has been found that man is naturally religious. We might be inclined to shout hosanna, but we must be sobered by the realization that it has also been found that man is naturally murderous and lecherous. So, leaving aside for the moment the matter of whether his religious bent is good or evil in itself, I repeat again that man in all times and climes has shown a predisposition to turn to something higher than himself. Originally the idea of height was interpreted rather literally. The sun, the moon, a volcano, lightning, stars—many things high and powerful were worshiped. We know now that all this was nonsense, but, my dear friends, we interpret it none-theless as a step in the right direction.

A woman wearing a mink coat stopped. Men nearby inhaled the disturbing aroma of her perfume, looked at her with sidelong glances, and wished unconsciously but fervently that she were more beautiful than in fact she was.

The night huddled down to listen.

The American flag set in a based pole by the curb gradually became dripping wet. Three or four umbrellas mushroomed out over the crowd.

If religion were crystal-clear, dear people, it would have little attraction for the ignorant. Of course I do not speak of present company. Our most profound yearnings are for those things which we can never quite attain, although there must always be maintained the illusion that with just a little more effort we might attain them.

Now one question that has vexed man down through the centuries, dear friends, is that concerning God and evil. Either God is able to prevent evil and will not, say the skeptics, or He is unable to prevent evil and is there-fore not all-powerful.

Well, you and I bridle at that sort of word-twisting, do we not, brethren?

Speak up.

Yes, yes. Amen.

Very well. But the question still remains. We do not answer it by burning at the stake the man who has asked it.

Holy smoke!

Are you aware, dear friends, that the question has never been adequately answered? Oh, there have been men who have *thought* they answered it, but the body of intelligent opinion disagrees with them. In the end those of us who are in the camp of religion have had simply to say that the question was unanswerable. We have therefore restated our basic assumptions about God and closed the meeting with a prayer and a bit of organ music or incense.

But all the mystery of this point, brethren, is from this night on a thing of the past.

That's right. I have discovered the truth and I shall relay it to you.

Hear, hear.

The perfumed woman, who had blue eyes, edged closer. Fee, Fie, Fo, Femme. The stars paused overhead, listening.

I will tell you the name of the earth.

And you will curse me for it.

Are you aware, my friends, that many of the great religions have buried somewhere in their theology the idea that man's present state is lower than a condition in which he formerly existed? You have heard of the fall? Of course. But have you the remotest conception as to just how far we have fallen?

Brace yourselves.

First, good people, might I take a survey among you? Would those of you who believe in hell, and by that I mean a place of fire and eternal torment, raise your hands?

What?

No hands?

Well, of course, a survey employing such a small sample is of questionable statistical importance, but I must say nevertheless that I am surprised. Or perhaps it is your reticence, your embarrassment at exposing your opinions in public, that accounts for this surprising result. Ah, well.

In the long run it is of not so much importance. But to return to the question as to how an all-good God can permit earthquakes and plagues and horrible accidents whereby innocent children are burned alive and unseemly wars between religions and congenital physical defects and insanities of all descriptions and the frightful list of all of man's woes—to return to that question, good friends, is my purpose now. I will tell you frankly that our God is all-powerful but that He has deliberately willed the evil that exists.

What? Why do you cry out against me?

Do not your fathers believe—nay, do not some of you believe in your hearts that God created the traditional hell of fire and brimstone? Is not this the supreme horror? Then what is so bad about thinking that He has created the sufferings of man on this earth?

But how is this compatible with the concept of His loving-kindness? I will tell you. I will explain a mystery that has never been explained before.

The two policemen had come back and were standing still now, listening, standing straight and dour in the rain.

A light wind whipped rain-spray across the faces of people who streamed past: gawking tourists; leather-jacketed youths, arrogant in the company of their kind; old women returning to solitary rooms in dismal off-Broadway hotels; lovers dazed by the sensuality of each other's nearness; young girls traveling in groups of three or four, flashing their eyes over the crowd with mixed modesty and brazenness, giggling and smiling and chattering as they walked and fought against the streaming crowd.

Under the ground the guts of the city boiled and hummed.

Religion, you have heard, is the opiate of the people. I tell you this is the grandest reason for its existence. How could we stand the daily torment, my beloved, if we had not something to kill the pain? Opium is not an evil thing in itself. It is only the use or misuse of it that can be called good or bad. And you will need a good strong dose to withstand the power of that which I am about to reveal to you.

I have learned where we come from.

Do you want to hear it? Can you stand the lightning blast of a sincere revelation?

Amen.

Stand back. Gentlemen, give the lady in the fur coat a little breathing room there.

We were once with God, dear friends.

Ah, the let-down. You wanted something more exciting. You already knew that, you say? It's in Genesis? I tell you it is *not*, although I do not choose to become distracted at this moment with a debate about the Bible. No, I mean what I say in a far more literal sense than Genesis intends, although you will note that it is no longer the fashion to interpret Genesis literally.

But I tell you, good people, what has been revealed to me in a dream, that we were once literally with God, in every full sense of the phrase.

It was not the angels, my friends, who committed the sin of pride and were cast out into darkness. It was man!

The larger of the two policemen reached inside his jacket and scratched his stomach.

A cab driver, angry at being cut off by a private car

at the corner, screamed, "Schmuck!" through his half-opened window. The word hung on the moist air. Some in the crowd laughed.

It was man himself and man alone who in the pure first state originated evil. You and I. Our mothers, our fathers, and our children.

It happened in an instant and in the same instant we decreed our own fate. We could no longer remain in the pure presence. The pure presence did not decide that. We decided it ourselves, inevitably. It was as simple and inescapable as a chemical reaction. Some of this and some of that equals automatically something else. That something else, my poor friends, that something else was our earth!

Horns blared and jazz music floated from the radios of passing cars. Thunder coughed distantly, in harmony with the rumble of a subway.

And now, dear people, the truth is practically all blurted out. Do you know your home? Do you know why you have never heard from those who have gone on, despite your cherished belief that they still live? Do you?

There is no life after the grave, except in the sense that some of us, for all I know, may have to come back and live through our suffering again. On that particular score I am not so certain, but this I do know: the name of the earth. Are you ready? Do you truly feel that you want to hear the rest of my message?

Very well.

We are standing this very moment, fellow sufferers, *in the pit of hades*. The name of our planet is Hell! That explains the reason for man's torment. That tells you why our history books are nothing more than ledgers of tragedy.

The luckiest among us, therefore, are those who have suffered the most in the shortest possible time.

A man standing close behind the perfumed woman touched her at this moment, his control lost. She whirled and slapped him. The policemen stepped in, collared the man, and when he resisted beat him into submission.

The red lights of Times Square twisted in torment on the glossy black asphalt.

11

Joe Shulman Is Dead

Joe Shulman is dead. We were sitting here in Nick's front room, in the Village, drinking, when Bill stepped out to take a phone call and then after a minute he came back in, waited till we stopped laughing at something, and said, "I don't mean to be a drag but Joe Shulman just died."

There was a flurry of soft "Oh, no's" and we all began frowning and looking at our drinks and the floor and the iced celery and carrots on the low, round white coffee table and at anything except each other's eyes.

I didn't actually know Joe intimately. He wasn't really what you would call a close friend, and yet he was the kind of man I would have liked to have for a good friend. It was only the business, the damned busy business, with its endless hustle and travel and meet and talk and decide and flip and then at last, as in Joe's case, die, before you had a chance to spend leisure time with the few people you met who seemed to be worth knowing better.

Joe was a bass player. String bass. He was my favorite. I wouldn't say he was the very best in the business, but for some reason I enjoyed playing with him the most. I play only moderately good jazz, but with Joe standing next to the piano, swinging back and forth with his eyes closing from time to time like a sleepy baby's, and his mouth framing a perpetual slight smile, I always played my best. Perhaps it was because I knew that he approved of what I was playing. Some bass players play for themselves, for their own enjoyment. Others are perfectionists who in a subtle way let you know that you're not quite on their level. But with Joe you always were supported by a combination of swinging, relaxed beat and a personal contact that let it be understood that besides being a musical experience your playing together was a type of warm social contact. There was a poetic sort of conversation that took place between his beat-up old bass and your piano. Mostly he played with his wife Barbara Carroll, but when you went to hear Barbara, if you were a pianist, she always asked you to sit in.

She is a fine jazz pianist herself, and she seemed to play her best after Joe joined her trio. I remember the general time; it was around 1953 and Jayne and I were still studying each other. Jayne's mother and father were missionaries. She was born in China and didn't see America till she was seven, so she was not like any other woman you might meet in New York. She didn't know the names of old movie stars, she didn't know the words of old songs, and she didn't understand jazz. All I knew about her at first was that she was beautiful and intelligent and the

kind of woman I wanted to invite into my world to become—well, to take over, actually. But I used to take her
to the jazz spots around town and explain the music to
her. She was a good student. One of the places I took
her to was The Embers on East 54th Street. We used to
sit close together at a table against the wall and I would
put my hand on her knee under the tablecloth and softly
tap out the rhythm of the music. I introduced her to
Barbara and Joe, and Joe seemed to take a particular interest in our romance. He would step over to the bar
and discuss with the bartender a very particular sort of
oversized martini and then he would bring two of them
back to our table and we would drink them and fall more
in love with each other and with the whole world. Alcohol
may be an evil thing if that's the way you feel about it,
but it is not entirely evil in that it can release in man a
certain capacity for universal love that otherwise fre-
quently remains locked deep within him and in some individuals never gets a chance to get to the surface at all.

So Joe would keep bringing these martinis to us and
he would laugh at my jokes and tell Jayne how beautiful
she was and I guess you might say that he was sort of our
Cupid. We would have eventually gotten married without
him, no doubt, but he surrounded the early days of our
courtship with an amber Embers haze of good feeling and
logs in the fireplace and hands across the table and laughter
and the deeply felt happy rhythm of good music.

I remember one time I was having dinner at the apart-
ment when Joe called me up and said that Barbara was
sick and he had a question to ask me and he figured I'd
say no but he was going to ask anyway, just for the heck
of it. He asked me if I'd like to fill in for Barbara at

the Embers for two nights and, man, it was ridiculous. I mean, here I was thinking it was the best invitation I'd ever had and he thought I'd say no. Anyway, I played there for two nights and Barbara thought I was doing her a big favor. Those two nights were a ball, and with Joe booming out the big fat beat hour after hour I felt that I was in good hands and it gave me the greatest possible confidence.

After Jayne and I got married we saw Joe rarely, but each time we ran across the Barbara Carroll trio it was a happy time. Usually it was by surprise. We'd be invited to a party at somebody's house and we'd be there talking and suddenly Barbara and Joe would come in and that meant that eventually somebody would open up the piano and Joe's bass would appear from some closet where he'd quietly slipped it when he'd entered and there would be music; and if I played I'd play far beyond my customary creative ability. Joe would lay down his rock-steady and yet unobtrusive beat and he'd keep smiling and whispering to me, like a father encouraging a child. He was young, about my own age, but as a musician he was much my senior, and he always made me feel that I was well taken care of when I was with him. Joe was an enthusiast: I guess that's the best thing anybody can say about him, and it's higher praise than it might seem at first thought. The world needs more enthusiasts. Most people are critics, putter-downers. Joe made you feel better than you were and as a result you *became* better. I'm sure he had experimented with drugs and ignored rather than consciously broken the Commandments, but by some sort of deep, elementary standard he was a good man. There was nothing vicious in him and yet he was the sort of person who

I'm sure would be criticized by people who consider themselves worthy but who are ever ready to bare their fangs.

Joe had a funny habit of closing his eyes when he played and doing a little stationary sort of dance, rocking back and forth within about a ten-inch arc, tipping his head first from one side then to the other.

I'm writing this now on a borrowed typewriter in a cubicle at Nick's house, while out in the front room the party rolls on. I'm enjoying the party, but I just had to step in here and put these few meager ideas on paper while they were on my mind. It was just a few minutes ago that Bill said, "Joe Shulman just died. Heart attack," and I don't fully understand the motivation that drove me in here to this little sweatbox and the Italian portable. I have my shirt and my undershirt off and just to my left on the table a cockamamie modernistic lamp is slanting its light through a low glass of scarlet wine. Maybe it's just a means of saying good-by to Joe, but damn it, there's no way of knowing that he's getting the message, and so I have the crazy idea that I ought to rush into the other room now and say to all of the gang in there:

"Listen, you're all going to die someday—soon or late—and it'll probably happen to some of you unexpectedly and to others when you've been scattered to a far corner, so don't think I'm too weird but I thought maybe I would say good-by to you now and tell you that I've really enjoyed knowing you and that I admire you. So now when you die you'll at least have had the glad hand from me. The way it happened to Joe and the way it happens to a lot of them, it's as if they were suddenly cut off while making a phone call. Joe was in his thirties and—oh, hell."

Naturally I won't say anything when I walk back in there.

It's sort of sad about the last time I saw Joe. I had to go to Chicago to meet with one of my sponsors a few months ago and after I checked into the Sherman I spent two days running back and forth to meetings and conferences and interviews. The second day, while leaving the old Medina Temple Building on North Michigan, I heard a voice that I thought had called my name. At that moment I was leaning forward to enter a taxi and a few seconds later, while the driver was making a U-turn, I glanced out the right-hand window and there were Barbara and Joe, smiling and waving. The driver slowed down a bit and I stuck my head out and yelled, "Where are you working?"

"The London House," Joe shouted. "Call us."

I said I would and then they were disappearing in the distance and I was rushing back to the Sherman house and the treadmill.

I never got to see Joe after that. Goddamn it. I don't know now that what I feel so maudlin about is him or what. Is it the realization that the world is just too much? Oh, God, why don't we walk around every single minute with our eyes wide open, drinking it all in, because it's being taken away from us little by little every day. I know now why some people believe in reincarnation: it has to be an idea born out of the same sense of incompleteness that I'm feeling right now as I sit here sweating and wishing I had more talent so I could tell you what I mean because, believe me, these words are doing nothing more than expressing the very vaguest outlines of my conception. Time runs out on all of us.

So what if I had lost a couple of hours' sleep on that last Chicago trip and gone over to the London House and listened to Barbara and Joe? I might have sat in and it would have been a ball, but it wouldn't have made the feeling of loss now any smaller. In fact, the better that now ever-lost evening would have been, the worse would be the present feeling.

Joe was young and he had blue eyes and light sandy hair and he was hip and relaxed and I swear that musicians at their best are a very fine type of people. I've never known a vicious musician unless he was a very bad musician. There's something about the business of playing that keeps a man young, younger than he would be if he were driving a bus or auditing in a bank. And that's why Joe died younger than even his years indicate.

To tell you what kind of a fellow he was, let me say first that the thing I do the very worst is play the clarinet. I took a few lessons once in connection with making a picture, and although every now and then I kid myself that I'll practice diligently for a couple of years and maybe eventually make it with the instrument, I actually realize that it takes eight or ten years to become good at it and that what with being busy and all, I'm never going to make it. But one night at a party at Bill's house I had a few drinks and the next thing I know I'm opening up the clarinet case and putting the plumbing together and somehow in my condition I have the idea that when I put the instrument in my mouth I'm going to play something worth while. It doesn't happen, of course. My tone isn't too bad for a beginner, but when you're handicapped by inadequate technical mastery of an instrument like the clarinet you're just handicapped, that's all.

But all of a sudden I'm playing, with Barbara at the piano and Joe at the bass, and I'm damned if they didn't make me play over my head. Nothing you'd care to hear again or talk about, of course, but still it's remarkable that I never played the clarinet that well before or since.

So that's about it. That's about all I know about Joe. I don't know where he came from or where he went to school or what his religion was or how he spent his time when he wasn't playing. All the moments we spent together probably wouldn't have added up to twenty-four hours. But let's work out the arithmetic that way. Let's put all the joking and the martini talk and the sitting-in and the swinging and the smiling and the understanding together and add it up to one twenty-four-hour period. And let's say it was one of the happiest days of my life. I owe it to Joe Shulman.

12

Hello Again, Darling

D<small>EAREST</small>, darling, sweet Marion,

January 12

Hello there again, you old sweetie-face. You were in great form tonight as usual. When Danny asked you to put the blindfold on and you complained that it would muss up your hair and then they took that big close-up picture of your face, do you know what I did? Well, you'll have to guess because if I told you what I did you might not want to meet me. Not that you've ever said it would be okay if we *did* get together, but I mean this was something pretty unusual and if you knew what it was why then you probably would feel embarrassed when we finally got to meet.

Anyway, there you were with your big old face on my TV screen and there was nobody here in the back of the shop but me and I gave you a great big kiss, you doll,

and that isn't all. They only had you on the screen in that
big close shot for a few seconds, but at least I got to kiss
you right on the mouth because I jumped out of my chair
the second you were there, real close like that, and I got to
the set quick as lightning and there we were together.

I still don't know, baby doll, when I'll get to come to
New York but it should be in a few weeks. My sister
keeps telling me I'm nuts but she should talk. That crazy
husband of hers works his—I mean (I musn't forget I'm
writing to a lady, must I, doll-face?). Anyway, Josephine
and Dom (that's her husband) have a pretty dull life if
you ask me and who did? He works overtime all the
time and all they do is fight and have kids. Not that it
isn't fun having kids (you know what I mean), but Josephine has to go through an awful lot of work after it's
all over. And if you *don't* know what I mean, you big old
doll-face, well, then, why don't you answer some of my
letters and meet me in Times Square next time I'm in New
York and we'll have a couple of drinks and talk things
over.

What I started to say was that Jo keeps telling me I
shouldn't write to you, but I've talked it over with this
doctor friend of mine and he says that as long as I'm not
doing any real harm well then maybe it's okay. I mean he
says it's okay if I write letters that you could show to that
lucky husband of yours. He says I shouldn't put anything
in the letters that I wouldn't be able to show to my mother,
but all I know is I never could show anything much to my
mother anyway, so to hell with that part of it. I always
figure that if my mother didn't know plenty, why I
wouldn't even be here now, so to hell with my mother.

You know what I'd like for us to do together, sweetheart? I'd like to get the train next Friday afternoon, the
one that gets you into New York about seven-thirty, and
I'd like to get off the train and then hang around Grand
Central for a while looking at all the pretty girls to sort
of, you know, get me in the mood for you, and then I'd
like to go have a drink at one of those smart-aleck "cock-
tail" lounges to sort of get a little more in the mood, and
then I'd like to give you a call at your home (if I knew
the number and I'm working on that, let me tell you) and
then you'd say okay, that we could get together and you'd
sneak out of the house or something so that that big strong
husband of yours wouldn't know where you were going,
and then you'd meet me someplace around Times Square
—like maybe in front of that burlesque theater near 42nd
Street where they have all those great pictures outside
(but nothing much inside, take my word for it), and then
we'd go someplace and have a drink and then, well, believe me, bright-eyes, the rest of the evening would be
something you'd never forget. I'd take my own close-up
of you with my eyeballs instead of that damned TV set of
mine that keeps going on the blink all the time. I got the
damned thing in 51 and I've gotten pretty sick and tired
of having the Jew bastard down the street fix it again
and again, and he keeps giving me a lot of jerky talk
about why the thing don't work and how he's giving me
a fair deal in the price of the repair work and all, but if
you ask me it's a lot of crap and one of these days I'm
gonna give him a punch right in his Jew mouth. So where
was I? Oh, yeah. Anyway, you and me, we'd go to one
of those Times Square hotels and we'd lock the door and,

baby, they wouldn't hear about us again for years. I mean
we'd keep right at it. I guess that's the sort of thing Dr.
Thorne keeps telling me I shouldn't write to you. I mean
that's the kind of remark I know that he's talking about,
although I've never actually said anything like that to him
and he hasn't come right out and used certain words to
me (you know what I mean), but he seems like a nice
guy and, what the hell, as long as he thinks he's doing me
some good I guess I might as well humor the old bastard
along and let him think that I'm making out. So if he
ever happens to get in touch with you, which God knows
he might do because he knows how much I care about you
and all and because he might come prying around and try
to find out what I keep writing to you about, why you
be a good kid, baby-face, and hand him some sort of a
stall but don't tell him about all this mushy stuff that I
keep writing to you.

Oh, I'm crazy about you, blondie. You know that, don't
you. There's a fat girl who works at a delicatessen near
here who jokes with me when I go in there once in a
while at lunch time to have a sandwich and I think she
likes me. But what the hell, she's a fat slob and once in a
while she wears sneakers and a man's sweater, you know
the kind, and what man in his right mind wouldn't rather
have Marion Green, the famous TV glamour girl? Well,
you know where I stand, kiddo. I mean this kid at the
delicatessen, her name is Roxanne, she ain't fit to polish
your shoes. I told her that I wrote to you and she told
me I was full of sauerkraut, and so just to prove to her
that I was on the level I showed her one of the letters. I
didn't show her the whole letter right off, you understand,
because a lot of this stuff is just between you and me,

you big old doll-face, you, but anyway I let her take a peek at a couple of pages and she got interested in what I was writing to you, so when she got to the bottom of one of the pages where it was getting sort of interesting because that was the letter I sent you last month where I was telling you how pretty I think your stomach is, why she got acting kind of peculiar and she says where's the rest of the letter? and I says why? and she says well, there must be more to it, that isn't the end and all, and I says why, sure there's more, but what business is it of yours? and she says why, none at all, she says, but she's curious just the same because it's only natural that anybody would be curious about anything that was left unfinished. So I reached into my back pocket and says here it is and re-member now that you insisted. I mean I didn't come in here and just offer to show you this letter and she said no, that's okay, let me see it. So I did and, sweetie-pie, you should have seen her blush. First she started to laugh and then when she got to the hot part she sort of giggled, and then she acted scared and she told me to get to hell out of the delicatessen and that I ought to have my head ex-amined for writing things like that, so I told her to go to hell and I walked out, which was actually a pretty good deal because I hadn't paid for my corned-beef sandwich and Pepsi Cola so I hope the old man made her pay for them herself.

Well, bright eyes, I guess that's about it for now. The guy I work for is grousing about me having some lettering to do on some more of these signs here, so I guess I'll knock off and close.

Yours till butter flies
GEORGE

Hello, again, darling,

It's me. Lover-boy. I kissed you again on your show this week. When the panel was trying to guess Pat O'Brien's secret they took that close shot of you and I really gave you a good one. You laughed and everything. I could tell you loved it. Boy, that husband of yours must really have something to hang on to a doll like you. I talked that part of it over with Doc Thorne and he says that it's none of my business and that if your husband has anything at all that keeps you after him it must just be a nice personality. I mean he says that it's the way two people can just talk together and have fun reading books and things that is the most important thing between two people. But if I was your husband we wouldn't waste much time reading books, let me tell you. Although come to think of it I have a couple of books that we might have fun reading together at that.

Just for fun do you know what I did the other night? I don't know what got into me but I proposed marriage to this gal I told you about before. You know, the one that works at the delicatessen. I took her out after work and we had a couple of beers and then when I walked her home we necked a little bit on her street, which is sort of dark because some kids broke a street light and the damned politicians that run this town aren't in much of a hurry to fix things like that as long as they are getting theirs. Anyway, I got this crazy idea because she wouldn't let me fool around, so I thought maybe if I got engaged to her that she would have to, you know what I mean. So she got kind of interested because I guess I'm the first fella that ever asked her to get married except that we got talking about it and she said she would want kids because it was against her religion to get married and not to have kids, so I said that was okay with me but today I talked it over with the doc and he said that he thought I was making a mistake to get married in my present condition, whatever the hell that means, and he said that if I went against his orders and got myself married that it would be a terrible thing to bring up kids with me like I am now, and I told him that I didn't know what he was talking about and that anyway whatever Roxanne wanted to do would be okay with me and that I wouldn't want to do anything against her religion and that I liked kids and he made some smart crack about religion and then suggested that we kind of change the subject. He asked about you and I told him that if I had my way I'd marry you instead of Roxanne and that would fix her wagon and his too for that matter. And you know, doll-face, I'd like to fix *your* wagon. I guess that's a dirty joke, isn't it? Some people keep telling me I shouldn't tell dirty jokes or say things like that but I say what the hell. That's freedom of speech, isn't it? You show me a guy who's afraid to tell a good dirty joke and I'll show you a real creep every time.

I discovered the other night how to make you blush, by the way, did I tell you? No, I didn't so here I go. I sit down on the floor here in the back of the shop and I sit right up close to the TV set, see, and then I put my hand on the knob on the left-hand side of the set, the knob that has to do with how dark or bright the picture gets and then when they take a good close picture of your face I say something real wild to you and then fast I give the knob a little twist and your face gets darker and it looks like you're blushing. The other night Danny was saying something to you there in New York and I didn't exactly hear what it was because I was saying something a lot more interesting to you myself, if you know what I mean, and I think any girl with a shape like yours must know plenty, sister, so anyway I said this real wild thing and I gave the knob the little twist and just then you looked real shocked because of what Danny said but to me it looked like you were making that face because of what I had said. Man, I laughed so hard I like to bust a gut. You and me were really on the beam that night.

I think next week when you're on I'll get a piece of tracing paper and put it over the screen and try real fast to draw your face. And then I can go on kissing you even after the program is off.

I guess you think that sounds sort of odd but love does funny things. Actually it makes me sad sometimes. I always write these letters to you like I hadn't a care in the world, and to tell you the truth I always make a special point to put a lot of jokes and funny stuff in these letters so you'll get a kick out of them and won't get sore at me and tell on me but to tell you the truth, Marion, I have a lot on my mind. I don't want to bother you with these troubles but ever since the court said I had to see Doc once a week the thing has sort of been bothering me. I guess I could drink like my old man, but to tell you the truth I just don't care much for the taste of the stuff. Oh, I like a drink if it's in Coke or lemonade or something but the taste of liquor itself I can do without. Which proves there's some hope for me, I guess. If you had the time why I bet you could straighten me out in no time. I bet you could take me to one of those fancy New York shops and help me pick out some nice clothes, that is if I had the money. Or if you want to "keep" me. (Joke!) And they say that clothes make the man. I believe that, I really do. This damned army jacket business certainly does nothing for my morale, that's for sure. Also I'm not the best-looking thing in town, but Doc says that doesn't mean a damn and he tells me the names of lots of guys who weren't exactly Rudolph Valentino in the looks department and still made out all right. Guys like Edward G. Robinson and Sammy Kaye and Albert Einstein and lots of other guys like that. So I'm sure you wouldn't hold my looks against me. Although I'd like to hold mine against you. (Joke again.) I'm pretty funny, don't you think. I've always thought that if I'd gotten the breaks I could have gotten into show business myself. I know Charlie, the guy I work for, always laughs at me. He's pretty stupid but he does laugh at me, that much I have to say for him.

Whee-hoo. I'd like to give you a kiss right now. You make me feel lots better just writing to you, writing about my problems and everything and believe me, sexy-face, I'm certainly grateful for that. If there's anything I can ever do to return the favor don't hesitate to call on me. You know the address so you just tell me what it is. I'll do anything for you and I do mean anything. And if anybody ever gives you any trouble you be sure to let me know. I'm not very big and I'm not particularly known as a tough guy but if I lose my temper as I once in a while do then, believe me, everybody better look out. I'm handy with a knife, that's one thing the goddamned army did for me and you just give me the name and the address of whoever is giving you any trouble, cutie-doll, and that'll be the end of them. Oh, don't worry, I don't actually suppose I would do anything reckless, you know what I mean, but I'd sure scare the hell out of them and they'd leave my girl friend alone from there on in, believe you me. I feel lots better tonight, Marion. Writing this letter has been great for me. I think I'll call up Doc and tell him to go jump in the lake. Who needs him? XXX!

Your happy warrior

GEORGE

13

The War

You have been kind to us. For that we are grateful beyond our power to express. Although you are by now familiar with most details of the story, I will try to tell you again how it was.

The enemy occupied the west, speaking in loose terms, and we held the east. It had not been planned that way; it was just that we occupied most of the large cities and when the exodus had begun, the newly homeless had fled, drawn by a sort of socio-geographic gravity, to the small towns and the open prairies and the relatively undeveloped areas. Once the trend had manifested itself, it seemed to grow of its own momentum. During the last few years before the outbreak of open warfare those of our people who had settled in the west had begun to drift back to the right-hand portion of our country; when the enemy perceived the turn events were taking, they correspondingly began to gather themselves together on our left. The war was not, it should be made clear, fought for such folly as, for example, the War Between the States during which men were made enemies by something as impersonal and meaningless as a boundary line between geographical areas. All war is folly, of course, but some wars more so than others. There was less of the comedy of tragedy than usual, I believe, in ours. Enmity had been growing for a considerable period of time, and the lines between the two camps were at last clearly drawn, unobscured by such trivia as rival ideologies, accidents of geographical placement, prejudicial racial attitudes, and the like. The issue was neatly cut.

But who can ever say exactly how a war starts? There is not one cause; there are dozens, perhaps hundreds. In our case while we were concentrating on one set of problems, another sneaked up and caught us unawares, so to speak. You have studied our history books and periodicals and you are familiar in general with the tensions and stresses of the period. But as is often the case with war, it was a peculiar problem that caused the first cleavage.

This issue of unexpected import, the point that eventually presented itself as the spark for the proverbial tinderbox, was the matter of birth control.

At the half-century mark some men had begun to worry about the problem of radiation. Five years later it was not uncommon to see articles in magazines and newspapers pointing out to the people that history, painfully developing a monstrous joke, might bring it about that what the press called the "atomic radiation peril" would be the true danger of the force of atomic energy, and not the expected explosive atomic war.

As we are now aware, the feared outbreak of hostilities never came to pass. The ideologies that seemed inevitably committed to instigate it gradually blended into each other, the democracies becoming more socialistic and the communist states becoming more democratic after the Russian revolution of 1977. But from Hiroshima on, the forces of fear and mistrust prevented any accord on international control of atomic energy, any mutually satisfactory method of arms inspection, and, in the end, the construction of any satisfactory mechanism for peace. But the war nonetheless never quite broke out. The bomb tests continued. X-ray and fluoroscopic examinations continued. The debate waged endlessly on the problems of fall-out, contamination, and genetic damage.

The first definite hint of things to come was noted in 1957 when a number of soldiers who had been exposed to radiation complained that several of their group had been made sterile and that some of the rest had fathered defective offspring. At first the noted defects were relatively slight: cleft palates, club feet, and the like. By 1965 more serious mutations were observed and the word "monstrosity" was being guardedly employed by medical authorities and the press.

In certain parts of the nation it happened that radioactive particles fell in heavier-than-average concentration, and wherever in these sections the land was chiefly apportioned to agriculture, the grasses and vegetables were discovered to have surprisingly high radioactivity. A few advanced scientists urged that a number of entire areas destroy their crops rather than offer them for sale, but in the end it appeared that economic considerations, which were susceptible to common understanding, carried more weight than scientific "scare talk," as one Senator called it. The result was that children in four states, because their growing bones filtered strontium out of greens and milk and retained it, suffered genetic damage. This was not clearly recognized at the time. It was only after 1970, by which time these youngsters themselves had reached the age where they could marry and reproduce, that it was observed that in these four areas, the number of badly formed and monstrous offspring was relatively large.

Birth-control advocates immediately came forward with the predictable suggestion that until the confusion surrounding the genetic question had been cleared up it would be most wise to limit childbearing. The churches, also predictably, put forth the classic argument that the end did not justify the means and that, if birth control was sinful at all, then it was sinful at all times except when it was accomplished by abstinence. The anti-birth-control forces printed large quantities of pamphlets explaining the rhythm method during this period. The people, accustomed to adopting attitudes and sticking to them, continued to hold to one side or the other according to historic balance and in direct relationship to religious affiliation or the lack of it.

It was not until several years thereafter, when some of the malformed and monstrous progeny themselves had grown to maturity, that the birth-control debate flared to white heat. Even some of the most devout began to hint that to allow the monstrous to marry and procreate was not to advance the cause of wisdom, not to mention ultimate national security. The magazines of the day were filled with articles on birth limitation, euthanasia, sterilization, and theology. For some, chiefly the old and the sterile, the time was one of a return to religion. For others it was a period of open iconoclasm. Groups identified as "liberal" promoted large amounts of money to pay for the distribution of anti-religious literature, and men on street corners were heard to quote Thomas Paine, Voltaire, Hume, Shaw, Ingersoll, H. G. Wells, Bertrand Russell, and others, while those with whom they so hotly debated recited from the Bible, the Papal encyclicals, Aquinas, Augustine, Luther, and their local pastors.

At first these debates seemed to be only religious in character, but with the passing of another five years a subtle change began to take place. The young defected in large numbers from the churches and began to move to new localities, chiefly the far southwest and northwest, which, it had been learned, were, paradoxically enough, less affected than easterly areas by the fall-out. Then, too, it was true that most industrial atomic equipment was concentrated in the east. The old, or more precisely those past the age of parentage, tended to stay put if they were in the east. Those of them who lived in the west began first in a trickle and eventually in a flood to head for eastern cities and for neighborhoods and particular dwellings formerly occupied by the young.

The pattern is by now familiar. The cold war smoldered, like a fire trying to break out under snow, for many years. Press attacks and public utterances by leaders on both sides became more heated. "The old," said youthful General Burke Collins, "mistake their apathy for sagacity. Because they no longer care passionately about the things that are important to the rest of us, they imagine that they have attained a peak of lofty wisdom. Well, they have another think coming!" The young more and more came to blame the old for the condition of the world, to become more irreligious, to press for planned peace with other nations, to seek for more material benefits.

The old became more impatient and took to scolding the young as if they were all children. The nation had two souls: that of the parent and that of the child. There were evidences of love between the two groups, of course, but the antagonisms were decidedly more pronounced. As always, bad news was given more attention than good. By 1985 it was apparent that a crisis was imminent. Families had ruptured, friendships had been broken; the familiar patterns of social insanity common to times of war had become clearly recognizable. There was suspicion between friends. The young were complaining that the old, instead of having the decency to die, were hanging on and passing their frustrations and complexes on to the new generation.

"Honor Thy Father and Thy Mother!" thundered President Rattigan.

"Let Rattigan keep order in his own house," retorted a spokesman for the young, Governor Harris of California, making capital of the fact that the President's son had broken with his father and openly avowed his willingness to support the cause of free-thinking youth everywhere.

Being eighty-seven years old at the time, my sympathies were naturally with those of my age group, but I will admit that there was right and wrong in both camps. For one thing, the science of geriatrics had progressed so remarkably that the national life expectancy had taken dramatic rises. It was no longer considered news that leading figures were living more than a hundred years. The papers and TV from time to time would comment if a man passed a hundred and twenty, but anything short of that was considered unworthy of special attention.

As a psychologist I regretted the opening of hostilities, but I do take a certain measure of rueful pride in having predicted the ultimate danger back in the '50's when as a young man I observed the widespread incidence of juvenile delinquency. The rebellion of the children was not, it should be borne in mind, only an American problem. All over the world, governments were faced with the thorny problem of handling surly teen-agers.

In my professional capacity, too, I felt particular sorrow when the showdown came, but I still am inclined to insist that we had no other course of action available to us. General Collins' insult to the few remaining veterans of the first World War was one of the last straws; the army rebellion at Fort Leonard Wood was another. Young officers simply relieved their older superiors of their desks and escorted them roughly to the camp gates. Readers are probably familiar with the news picture of the unseemly fist fight that occurred between General Allan and a young colonel on this occasion. It was a time of open defiance. We had to drop the first bomb.

For months, older Air Force officers had been taking refresher courses and top missile brass had been busy refamiliarizing themselves with details that had perhaps for too long been left to underlings. But we were handicapped in this area. The only course open to us, as I say, was to take the initiative. It was either that or risk immediate annihilation.

The young people simply wanted us to die. They had said precisely as much. My own son had written it in a letter. "You must realize," he had said, "that the problem of overpopulation cannot be solved by birth control alone. We are doing our part, but you cannot ask us at this late date to remain childless, by whatever means. It is up to you to make the move. You have become the unwanted guests at the party. It is all over as far as you are concerned, but you have not the grace to go home. You are eating food, drinking water, and breathing air that was intended by nature for growing children. You have concentrated the wealth and frozen power in high places. Your hand grows palsied on the throttle but you will not relinquish control. Please have the decency to die."

While the attitude was spiteful and generally unjust, a fair-minded man would have to admit there was at least a particle of sense to their argument. The nation, especially the eastern part of it, was badly overcrowded. True, there were a few wild and undeveloped areas remaining in the west, but they were largely uninhabitable. Telling a man raised in New York or Boston or Chicago that he must now suddenly build a home with his bare hands in the mountains of Colorado or on the Arizona desert was obviously not to solve the basic problem. The nation had progressed too far technically to justify a frontier existence of the sort associated with the previous century.

The young embarrassed us terribly after we dropped the first bomb. Although we selected a relatively uninhabited area of Oregon as the target for the first missile, there were nevertheless hundreds of people killed. We demanded immediate surrender on the basis that, although both sides had bomb stockpiles, ours was by far the larger and that any contest on that basis would only lead to general disaster on the one hand or victory for us on the other.

The young charted a wise course at that point in turning to the rest of the world and sending up a cry for judgment. "We decline to retaliate in kind," they said. "It was this bomb created by our fathers that was largely responsible for our early and present troubles. We will not pick up this disgraceful weapon. Rather, we will resort to the arms created and popularized in more humane times. We will use planes, old-fashioned explosives, missiles, light, medium, and heavy weapons, tanks, and infantry. We will fight a war to the death if need be, but there is one weapon we will not use."

Fine words, but alas they were more characteristic of the first days of the war than the last. Wisdom, even of the most relative sort, has never yet in man's long history been the ultimate master of passion. We pressed all men between sixty and eighty-five into our service at once and provided our troops with special medical care to insure their function at peak efficiency. As soldiers, most of our forces were inexperienced and slovenly, but as men they were remarkably strong and determined. Their age armed them with a peculiar sort of spiritual authority and our leaders sought constantly to appeal to them on this level with, I scarcely need add, considerable success. In hand-to-hand combat, of course, our troops were hardly a match for the enemy, but war had come to be a business that involved very little hand-to-hand fighting. We were heavily mechanized and perfectly armed, since most munitions factories were in our control. Needless to say, the discoveries of cures for various types of cancer and prevention of most heart ailments had insured that our forces would be superior in number. Also it must not be forgotten that in resorting to the limitation of their families the young had played into our hands.

The war raged for several months with the outcome very much in question before Canada and Mexico were drawn in. Our second atomic missile, exploded over the young's munitions center, San Diego, had caused damage in Mexico. Within a week, fighting had broken out beyond both our borders. Within six months the third World War was under way, with national boundary lines, for the first time in history, having no meaning.

This was also the first time in history that no one side actually won a war. There was much suffering in both camps. The earth was a madhouse for the next several years. I fully realize that readers on this planet will be inclined to give little sympathy to us, newcomers in your midst as we are, and foolhardy as our past actions have undoubtedly been; but in frankly confessing our past errors I feel that we are giving indication at least of our good faith. We have not come among you with warlike intentions, and your openhearted acceptance of us has proved that you take us at our word.

Your insistence that we leave our weapons on earth has, as you know, met with our complete approval, for it is well known that no one hates war like an old soldier. Our children drove us from our home and we are strangers among you, but you are restoring warmth to our hearts and for that we are sincerely grateful. For my part there is no enmity left in me for the enemy, no demand for revenge. After all, each year millions of the enemy are forced to leave their camp and defect to our side, so to speak, by the simple and inexorable process of aging. As you have seen, we are living at peace with these latecomers to your planet. Indeed, after they are here a short time it is difficult to distinguish these foreigners from those of us who came over on the *Mayflower*, if I may inject a small note of humor into this serious dissertation. Their coming has even reunited families that were torn apart many years ago by the brutal hand of war. Your life is strange to us. Your flowers have a strange smell and your food lies heavily in our stomachs. But your sky is clear and peaceful. For that we are grateful.

14

Dialogue

SHE: I love you.

HE: Now that's what I call a good sensible greeting.

SHE: Do you think any of this is sensible?

HE: No.

SHE: Is anyone apt to notice your car?

HE: Certainly. Everyone who passes it.

SHE: Don't joke. I'm too nervous.

HE: That's part of it, of course. Perhaps it's a more important part of it than we realize.

SHE: There's no point in your standing there leaning in as if you're asking directions. Get in and drive; my hands are sweaty on the wheel.

HE: All right. Which way shall we head?

SHE: Oh, God, I don't know. Just drive around while I try to get myself under control.

HE: Don't try too hard. I don't want you under control.

SHE: Do you think the dark glasses make me look more conspicuous than I might without them?

HE: No, keep them on. Even without your false eyelashes your face is too well known.

SHE: I only have until five-thirty. Bill thinks I'll be on the lot till then.

HE: No matter how much time there is, it's never enough, is it?

SHE: No.

HE: Sit closer to me.

SHE: Like this?

HE: Yes.

SHE: Don't drive too fast.

HE: I'm not.

SHE: Where are we going?

HE: To a lovely place I've discovered. The Sordid Arms. Very close to the intersection of Adultery Boulevard and Clandestine Lane.

SHE: Harry, please.

HE: The words make you wince, eh? It's strange. People will put their heads down and bull their way through almost any sort of adventure that suits their fancy, but if it happens to be something that either is or seems improper, why, the last thing they want in the world is to hear the correct terminology for the business they're engaged in.

SHE: All right. Turn around.

HE: What?

SHE: I said turn around. Take me back to where you left your car and we'll call it a day.

HE: We'll do nothing of the sort.

SHE: Then please be—gentle.

HE: I'm sorry, sweetheart. Perhaps I can change the subject. No, I can't, really. But I *can* make my discourse less personal. I remember a case once . . . fellow I knew. He told me that he had cast off every last shred of his religious convictions (he was a Catholic, I think) but that he still could not bring himself to use the name of the Lord in vain, as the saying goes, except when he lost his temper. And when that happened he would feel bitter remorse. Whoops.

SHE: Why whoops?

HE: I called his remorse bitter. Cliché.

SHE: You can't help talking to yourself, can you?

HE: I don't consciously talk to myself; it's just that I can't break myself of the habit of listening to what I say. Curse of being a writer, I suppose.

SHE: You don't look like a writer.

HE: Lately I haven't been writing much like one either.

SHE: That's not true. *The Silver Sword* was topnotch.

HE: I'll tell you a secret. Arthur did the bulk of the work. That's why I refused to flip a coin with him for the Oscarino. I insisted he keep it full time. And if I don't look like a writer, what *do* I look like?

SHE: I don't know. Either a baseball player or a . . . a doctor maybe.

HE: You're casting. I think that in reality people rarely look like what they do for a living. It's just that Hollywood has adopted a certain sort of casting custom that has convinced us all that truck drivers look like Victor McLaglen and diplomats look like Walter Pidgeon and so forth.

SHE: I have dummy luggage in the trunk.

HE: Who will we be this time?

SHE: Who were we last time?

HE: Mr. and Mrs. Arnold Gage of Denver, Colorado.

SHE: Do you think we look like Denver, Colorado?

HE: We'll pass.

SHE: I hope so.

HE: Sweetheart, if you think for one minute that the money-hungry proprietors of these motels don't realize that a certain almost fixed percentage of their customers are not truly man and wife——

SHE: God, that makes it seem worse.

HE: What do you mean?

SHE: If they *know* that two per cent . . . or ten per cent or thirty per cent . . . or whatever it is . . . that a certain number of us are only men and women looking for a place to sleep together, why, then they must look at all their customers with a suspicious eye.

HE: So? What if they do?

SHE: Doesn't it make you feel guilty?

HE: No. Oh, I feel guilty all right, but I'll be damned if I care what some sleazy retired farmer in a wrinkled shirt thinks of me. I feel guilty unto myself, you might say.

SHE: Well, I'm glad to hear that. I was beginning to think you were treating all this too lightly.

HE: I love you. I'm sorry you're forced to think so many unhappy thoughts because of this——

SHE: Oh, don't worry about me. You're not holding a gun to my head. No one is forcing me to see you. By the way, what time do you have? My watch has stopped, I think.

HE: Getting near four. I was waiting back there for over twenty minutes. What took you so long?

SHE: The damned hairdresser. She did my hair so badly that we ran late shooting the stills.

HE: You look beautiful.

SHE: Thanks.

SHE: I'll take my lipstick off. Look more like Denver.

HE: Good idea. And you might try the bandanna thing on the head.

SHE: All right.

HE: Here we go. Ah, good. Only one other car on the parking lot. I'll pull in back here. You can sit in the car and wait while I check in.

SHE: All right. Hurry. I think I liked it better the time you had the room already booked and we just parked and went in.

HE: Sorry. Didn't have time. The low heels are a good idea, by the way. Somehow you look much more virtuous in low heels.

SHE: Stop that.

HE: That's my girl. Be right back.

HE: There. All's well.

SHE: Fine. Where do we go?

HE: B-Five. Right up these stairs. I'll get the bags out of the trunk.

SHE: My heart is pounding.

HE: Relax.

SHE: It's such a clear, beautiful day. Why couldn't it be foggy or dark? People wouldn't be so apt to recognize me.

HE: Forget it. People won't recognize you here for the

simple reason that they don't expect to see you in a place like this.

SHE: Did you see those children playing on the sidewalk out front?

HE: Yes. What about them?

SHE: They looked at the car as we drove in.

HE: Naturally. It's a good-looking car.

SHE: B-Five. Is this the room?

HE: Yes. Here we are. All the comforts of home.

SHE: Lock the door.

HE: Done.

SHE: I love you.

HE: I love you.

SHE: It's silly, but every time we're in a place like this . . . no matter what it looks like, I get the crazy idea that it's our home and that I've got to fix it up so you'll like it and that I've got to run down to the store and get groceries and everything.

HE: That sounds like love all right.

SHE: I'm afraid so.

HE: You haven't given any more thought to divorcing Bill?

SHE: No. I don't know why, but I just couldn't do that to him.

HE: You're doing this to him.

SHE: He doesn't know about this.

HE: What if he were to find out?

SHE: It would kill him.

HE: You're being very literal.

SHE: I'm afraid I am. I don't know if his heart could take it. It took him so long to get over the last attack. There musn't be another.

HE: There will be sometime.

SHE: But it mustn't be for many years. Till he's had his share of years.

HE: Is he happy with you?

SHE: I think he is. And as I've told you . . . I do love him.

HE: I know. Strangely enough, I'm not jealous.

SHE: That's something. Although I almost wish you were.

HE: Now who's joking? But it is funny when you think of it. In the past I've always been easily inclined to jealousy. This time . . . believe me, I do love you. Very much. But I don't mind the idea of Bill. Whatever he has with you, I'm sure it's not the same as the thing we have together.

SHE: That's true.

HE: Of course, no two relationships are ever the same. But enough of that. I think I'll take a shower.

SHE: All right. Leave the door open. I want to hear you splashing.

HE: You're beautiful.

SHE: Thank you.

HE: I don't know what it is, but looking at the back of your neck makes me very excited. I want you.

SHE: Darling.

HE: I cannot stop telling you how beautiful you are.

SHE: Are you sure the door is locked?

HE: Yes. Forget about the door.

SHE: I keep thinking of the children.

HE: What children?

SHE: The ones who were playing on the sidewalk as we drove in.

HE: When you look at yourself in the mirror, aren't you absolutely astounded at your own beauty?

SHE: No.

HE: Then you have no taste.

SHE: If you must know, I've never been happy with the way I look. I always wanted to look like somebody else.

HE: Who?

SHE: Oh, no one in particular. I'm too catty for that. But just, you know, stray faces seen in the night. Girls I knew in school. Faces you see on the blank-looking models in *Vogue*. Perhaps Garbo. Somebody. I don't know.

HE: And to think of the millions who look at you on the screen and want to look like you.

SHE: That's life.

HE: You're a philosopher.

SHE: Don't tease me. Kiss me.

HE: Funny you should mention that. Ah, angel, what is it that brought us together?

SHE: Well, you sound very sad.

HE: Do I? I suppose I am. Why is it that when I'm with you I want to talk my head off, to tell you the most pointless things?

SHE: Pointless?

HE: Well, for example. You see that copy of *Time* that somebody left on that table over there? Well, I want to tell you that I've been reading *Time* for twenty years or so, but I've never once in all those years read that little section up near the front of the magazine . . . that department labeled "Letter from the Publisher."

SHE: That's funny. I never have either.

HE: You see how it is. Here we are laughing at something that's inconsequential. I know many handsome women. The studio abounds with them, swaggering past my offices, with their tight skirts and their thin ankles, and yet I have no desire to sleep with them because I know from the first that they will not be interested in what happened to me in kindergarten and they will not be interested in my telling them that most people mispronounce Dylan Thomas' first name and—do you understand?

SHE: Perfectly. I feel the same about you. I have been married to Bill for twelve years and in many ways we have a wonderful relationship. But—well, to sum it up, after Bill makes love to me, life just gets right back on the track and goes its merry way. After you and I make love we lie and talk.

HE: Yes, we do. But aren't we rather putting the cart before the horse today?

SHE: Yes, it's getting late. Kiss me.

HE: I love you.

HE: I never got to that shower. I'll try it now.

SHE: All right.

HE: I can see a little stripe of blue sky through the window in here.

SHE: Are you cold?

HE: No, fine, thanks. The fresh air feels good.

SHE: Leave the water running for me when you're through.

HE: All right.

HE: Don't dress just yet. Lie here. In my arms.

SHE: All right.

HE: It's funny, the point you made a little while ago, about our talking after we make love. I feel like talking.

SHE: What do you feel like saying?

HE: Is it possible to feel like talking and yet have nothing to say? I think it must be. I know I've often raced to my typewriter, full of the most wonderful feeling that I had something important to get out of me, something vital to get down on paper, only to discover that I had the inclination but not the substance, not the real wherewithal. Perhaps inspiration is what happens when the mood and the idea come at the same time, if you'll pardon the expression.

SHE: Oh! You'll joke on your deathbed.

HE: Come to think of it, that expression *should* be pardoned. It's such inept wordage. It's like the phrase "to make love." You don't really make love when you engage in sexual intercourse. The phrase has a sort of pidgin-English sound to it. Native boy, native girl, they get together, make love.

SHE: Wouldn't it be wonderful if we had some sort of moral standard that was uncomplicated?

HE: What the hell are *you* talking about?

SHE: What?

HE: Well, I'm talking about one thing and you're talking about another.

SHE: I'm sorry.

HE: Now you sound hurt.

SHE: I'm not.

HE: Yes, you are. I didn't mean to offend you. It's just that I was—oh, hell. I'm sorry. You're quite right if you did take offense. I was rude. But then, I *am* rude.

SHE: You are not.

HE: Oh, yes I am.

SHE: All right. We can drop it. What happened was that you were talking about pidgin English and all that and I got to thinking about the uncomplicated morals of the primitive society.

HE: And what do you think about it all?

SHE: That it's too bad our civilization is so complicated. We seem to have such a long list of sins, just as we have a longer list of machines and social customs and——

HE: So it's your conscience again.

SHE: Yes. I'm sorry. I can't help it.

HE: Well, if you can't beat 'em, why not join 'em?

SHE: What do you mean?

HE: I mean recognize what you're doing and say to hell with it. I mean accept what we're doing as the thing that you want or that you can't do without.

SHE: That sounds terribly cold-blooded. I'm not that modern.

HE: Perhaps it's not modern at all. Perhaps it's a very primitive attitude that I'm suggesting.

SHE: I don't know. God, none of us know much, do we? We learn a little each day, if we're lucky. Or if we're unlucky. Anyway, we learn a little each day and along about the time we've got things fairly well figured out, it starts to get dark out and we've lost interest in the game. And the personal, valuable things we learn never seem to get put down on paper, somehow, so that we can pass them on to our children. Or if they do get put down on paper they sound embarrassing to the young . . . or ridiculous . . . so that they are ignored, and in the end each person has to go through it all himself and learn it all privately and painfully.

HE: Bull.

SHE: What?

HE: I just said that to see if you were paying attention, as the comedians say. I said that once to a choir master when I was fourteen and got kicked out. But I say to your conscience to go jump in the lake.

SHE: Why?

HE: Perhaps because I'm jealous of it. I'm not jealous of Bill but I'm jealous of your conscience. Because I think your conscience could separate us, while Bill could not.

SHE: My conscience isn't just mine. It's my society's.

HE: I don't think so. If that were true, everybody would have the same conscience.

SHE: Don't they?

HE: Not by a long shot. In his secret heart, everybody's a Protestant. Even the most orthodox have their individual eccentricities. But we must conform, and I'm getting pretty sick of that word too.

SHE: What word?

HE: Conform. Conformity. It's *the* word just now. Everybody starts to say the same thing about conformity and then after a while somebody gets up and says something that opposes the new trend. *Right* and *wrong* or *useful* and *useless* are concepts that are almost cast aside. The debate simply rages for its own sake, I think. Controversy is terribly stimulating to man. What is it, a substitute for physical aggression? Unfortunately, it *leads* to physical aggression in many cases. I think I'll kiss you again.

SHE: Please do. Here we are, snuggled together. Two little amateur philosophers saying things we're not sure we believe.

HE: Don't knock that. That's what's so wonderful about the combination. I don't talk like this when I'm alone or with other people, really. You just seem to be a magnet, a sponge that soaks ideas out of me. You make me talk a certain amount of foolishness, I'm sure, but you also pull some worth-while ideas out of whatever the hell mechanism in my head produces all this gobbledygook.

SHE: I love your long arms.

HE: I love everything about you.

SHE: Is the guilt I feel part of the attraction of all this?

HE: I think we've gone over that one before. The answer is "absolutely," from the picture *Ill Wind*. It's a hypocritical world, my chesty wench, and the trouble isn't so much that everybody's wrong as it is that everybody's right.

SHE: What do you mean? I seem to keep saying that. Like a straight man.

HE: For which I am indebted. You only save me the trouble of asking myself the same question. Well, I'm not sure what I do mean, but if I keep on talking I may find out. Let's see now. What is it that's troubling you, pretty-mouth? You feel sinful, isn't that it? Isn't that hitting it right on the head? You're worried about the old scarlet letter. You're worried about sin. Well, let's see now. Let's just kick this mother around and see what comes out.

SHE: You're not going to defend sin, are you?

HE: I accept your challenge, madame. Is it the conventional thing to knock sin? Well, I won't go along! That is, not completely. I say give the devil his due. Let's take inventory. Pride, covetousness, lust, anger, gluttony, envy, and sloth. The big seven. There they are . . . engraved on stone in capital letters. Or neatly indexed, as you will, for clergymen to make pat sermons about. Christianity always has seemed to feel that if you identified a sin . . . gave it a name . . . you were halfway home in overcoming it. In that respect I suppose the early church fathers were much like the modern psychiatrists. Give something a name. Wrap it up in a box. That way you can sink tongs into it and throw it around. Well, to hell with all that. What's *wrong* with pride? It's a black sheep. It has to shift for itself while everybody praises love. Love is the spoiled child. I say pride is responsible for more material progress, more meat-and-potatoes advancement, than love ever was. It's evil pride that makes us want to come out on top, to have the best clothes, the best children, the best religion, the best city, the best nation, the best world. It's pride that even makes us look worse sins in the face and tell them where to get off.

Covetousness? Well, here again Christians go around quoting the Master. If you would be perfect, give up what you have and come follow me. And not one in ten billion has ever done it. No, sir. We may criticize poor covetousness, but that's just for show. Secretly we're all in love with her. She builds up our bank accounts. She puts shoes on our children. She moves us to a better neighborhood, helped—never forget—by pride. And the churches that preach the blessedness of the poor from their golden altars . . . it's a joke.

SHE: Everything is a joke with you, isn't it?

HE: Of course. If life weren't a joke, how could we stand it? What's next now? Lust. Why, that word is the biggest joke of all, possibly. The world has two choices. Lust or dust. Either we lust or we perish. Do you want to give it other names? Do you want to call it love too?

Go ahead. There's nothing wrong with that. But don't try to deny lust its rightful place. I lust. You lust. He lusts. We lust. You lust. They lust. The worms in the earth and the birds in the skies lust. So why not we? Oh, I don't say we shouldn't subject it to a sort of logic and control, at least insofar as is in our pathetic power, but for God's sake, don't brand it with a hot iron. Don't make it a dirty name.

SHE: There are unclean forms of it.

HE: There are unclean forms of *everything*. But I say that even in its vilest form it's got elements of beauty and the wild striving of man through nature to something better than he has.

Anger. That's next on our list. Anger. Oh, your poor philosophers grant anger a place all right, but to turn the trick they simply call it *just*. Just anger. I'm angry now and to me my anger seems fairly dripping with justice. But it may not seem so to you. Does the condemned criminal like the taste of the just anger of the society that sends him to the slaughterhouse? Anger is as anger does. It can do evil or it can do good. Hell, how is *evil* anger to be successfully combated in this world if not with *just* anger? The turn of the cheek may be a pretty figure of speech but I'll tell you something: I've never yet seen it in the world of reality! No, wait. Come to think of it I *have* seen a cheek or two turned here and there. And always for one reason. Fawning cowardice. When you are weak—when to strike back would be to court certain disaster—why, then I'll grant it's wisdom to turn your cheek. That's not just Christianity. That's plain old-fashioned horse sense. But when my fellow men are as strong as the enemy, or think they are—or when (God help the enemy) they are even stronger—why, you could search the universe over for a turned cheek.

SHE: Have you a good word, too, to say for gluttony?

HE: I'm full of good words. You know the reason for gluttony, don't you? The psychologists tell us it's because there's not enough love to go around. So it's love's fault, for making itself so goddamned scarce that there's so——

SHE: You're being ridiculous.

HE: But of course. That, however, is a digression. I abhor digressions. If I had my way my life would be just one long conversation, lasting a million years, not permitting one single digression to deter me from discovering it all, from exploring every cranny that might hide one of God's secrets. I'm a glutton, you might say, for knowledge.

SHE: But what do you do with your knowledge?

HE: Why must I *do* anything? Ah, you're a child of a utilitarian age. You can't help it. Well, I can. I can fight it, or try to. I say that knowledge, like all forms of virtue, is its own reward. The whole world is a Chinese puzzle, don't you understand, and it's fascinating . . . it's wonderful *fun* just to figure it out. At least it is for me. So here's to gluttony too. The poor souls who aren't loved enough have to swallow something. And to be even more facetious, if you will, our entire Western economy is geared to gluttony. Have you the faintest conception of what would happen if we all went on the diet of the Christian ascetic? Why, there would be the greatest depression mankind has ever known. Wineries would close. Farmers would be ruined. Dairies would become weed patches. Bakeries would close down. The sellers of meat would be put out of business. The heart would be cut out of our economy. That great and all-powerful influence of our civilization, advertising, which supports the press, would totter and crumble. You cannot open a magazine or turn on a television set without being urged to gluttony. More. More. *More.* That's our world summed up in one syllable.

SHE: You *twist* everything. You make everything seem——

HE: Ah, no. It's true that everything is twisted, but *I* didn't twist it. Now, you take envy. Poor envy has a *very* bad name. Not a friend in the world. Oh, yeah? Well, I'll rise to her defense.

SHE: "Her," you say. Why do you use the feminine?

HE: Oh, please. Don't become a significance-attacher. There might well be significance of some sort to everything, but it's a pointless bother being concerned with all of it. You can become so addicted to attaching significance to things that you can spend the rest of your life like the proverbial Hindu mystic contemplating the navel of your utterance. Where was I? Oh, yes. Envy. Why, it goes hand and hand with pride. The two are linked inseparably. Is there a skyscraper here that's eighty-five stories high? Don't go away. Stand and watch. Before long you shall see envy build one over here that's ninety-five stories high. Is there a man with a million dollars? Envy will soon bring him a neighbor with two million. Is there a church in this neighborhood with a thousand communicants? Envy will make a rival sect expand to match it. Honey-pants, the case for envy is perhaps the very easiest of all to make out. Envy is not only admirable, in its way; I would venture to say that it has been indispensable to civilization as we know it.

SHE: And sloth.

HE: The first known reference to sloth is: "And on the seventh day He rested."

SHE: Blasphemy!

HE: You're very good at naming things, you know. You're like those little boys who stand on street corners and name automobiles. A car drives by. "That's a Chevvy," one of them says, and feels puffed up with pride. But to return to the point. Sloth is also indispensable to our civilization. Haven't you heard of the leisure class? To become a member of it is to achieve the highest ambition of our time. Why your swimming pool and mine? Why all the labor-saving devices? Why all the dishwashers and automatic ironing boards and gasoline-powered lawn mowers and hammocks and sleeping pills and servants and all the rest of it if we aren't absolutely *dedicated* to sloth?

SHE: Very well, counsel for the defense. You've made out a case for the sins. Whether it's a good or bad case I'm perhaps not intelligent enough to judge. Now, will you assume another role? Will you be prosecuting attorney and put the virtues on trial?

HE: That will have to wait for another day. I'm tired.

SHE: What time is it? Oh, dear. I'm late.

HE: We'll be out of here in three minutes. It won't take you long to drop me at my car.

SHE: All right.

HE: The sun is still shining.

SHE: Beautiful day.

HE: Where did I put the key?

SHE: There. On the dresser.

HE: Oh, yes.

SHE: I think the water is still dripping in the shower.

HE: It will be all right.

SHE: When will I see you?

HE: I can't say. Soon.

SHE: All right.

HE: I'll leave the key right here. I'll take the bags down. You can follow right behind me in case anyone happens to be looking.

SHE: Right.

HE: It's gotten a bit cooler.

SHE: Just a little. Oh-oh.

HE: What's the matter?

SHE: Those children are still down there. Stay close to me.

HE: Don't worry. Here. Jump in. I'll throw the bags in the back seat. Save time.

SHE: Hurry.

HE: Let's see. Where is that key?

SHE: Upstairs.

HE: No, I mean the car key.

SHE: It must be in your jacket.

HE: Doesn't seem to be.

SHE: You'll find it. Don't be nervous.

HE: I'm all right. Where the hell *is* that thing? I'll have to get out of the car to check my pants pockets.

SHE: All right.

HE: Isn't that the damnedest thing?

SHE: Oh, God.

HE: What's wrong?

SHE: Here come the children. They'll recognize me. Can't you find the key?

HE: I'm looking. Put your glasses on.

SHE: That won't help. If they recognize me, there's no

telling what might happen. They'll blab it all over the neighborhood that I've been here.

HE: I'll tell them to go away.

SHE: No, that will look suspicious.

HE: I wonder if I left the key upstairs?

SHE: I don't know. Don't go up. I mean don't leave me alone here with those children. One of them . . . the tall girl . . . looks twelve or thirteen. She'll *know*, I tell you.

HE: Not a chance; stop worrying! Which girl do you mean?

SHE: The one walking this way. The one with the autograph book.

15

The House in Bel Air

When they got out of the limousine at the airport, a uniformed TWA man stepped up and said, "Miss Lane?" Harry Sonnenberg said, "Yes," as he helped Cora out of the car.

"As soon as you check in," the man said, "you can go right aboard."

"Thank you," Cora said, adjusting her sun glasses. She walked into the waiting room and paused momentarily at the ticket counter.

"You go ahead with the fella," Harry said. "I'll take care of all this. See ya in a minute."

When she had disappeared into a private lounge behind the counter, a photographer approached Harry. "Would Miss Lane mind posing for a quick shot waving bye-bye?" he said. "TWA."

"No, it's all right," Harry said. "No cheesecake this time."

"Fine," the man said, looking disappointed.

Cora posed for the picture, smiling blankly, then turned to climb the steps into the plane. Somebody whistled as the night wind whipping across the field pressed her mink coat tightly against the roundness of her hips, and she turned and smiled again in an impersonal, practiced way.

When Harry had put her overnight bag in her berth, he handed her the Los Angeles papers.

"You all set?" he said.

"Fine, thanks," she said. Harry was painless, colorless, odorless, tasteless: the perfect man for his job, which was putting actresses on airplanes, meeting them when they got off, pacifying columnists, handling the million-and-one minor details of publicity for the studio.

Before the plane had reached the Nevada-California border, Cora was ready for bed. She took a sleeping pill, accepted a glass of champagne from the stewardess who served nightcaps, allowed herself to be talked to flirtingly by a producer from another studio who happened to be on the flight, and turned in. Lying in her berth with her knees up, she read the funny papers and the gossip columns till her eyelids became heavy.

She slept soundly.

In New York she suffered through a three-day whirlwind of pictures, interviews, night clubs, theaters, appointments at the hairdresser's, appointments at the beauty parlor, and one appointment with a doctor, to see if she was pregnant. She was not.

The next morning a man from the studio home office

took her in the conventional Cadillac limousine to the airport and put her on the United Flight for Chicago.

"Well," he said when he had made her comfortable, "I'll bet you'll be glad to relax for a few days and see your family, eh?"

"Yes," she said.

"Somebody will meet you at the airport in Chicago," he said.

The man who met her three hours later was new at the job and seemed embarrassed, but he handled the baggage and saw her to a suite at the Ambassador East for which the studio had made the arrangements.

After he had left she called the house. Her mother's voice sounded harsh.

"It's me, Mom," Cora said.

"Oh, hello, angel," her mother said. "Where are ya?"

"I'm in town, at a hotel."

"Oh, my God, we woulda met ya. I thought you were coming tomorra."

"Didn't you get the last wire? Oh, never mind. Anyway, I'm here."

"Wonderful. Listen, I'll have Tom drive downtown after he gets off at the yards and pick you——"

"No, Mom, don't bother," Cora said. "I'll have somebody bring me out. Don't worry about that."

"It's no bother," her mother said. "Tom would love to do it."

Cora felt a knot in her stomach.

"Mom," she said, "will you listen? I don't *want* Uncle Tom to pick me up. I'll come out as soon as I can. Myself."

"All right," her mother said, "but I think you're crazy.

Tom would just love to drive down there and get ya. You must be dead, traveling and all, and it wouldn't take him more than twenty minutes on the outer drive to——"

"Listen," Cora said. "How is everybody? I mean how are you all?"

"Oh, we're fine, Marge," her mother said. Hearing her real name was always a shock to Cora, although a very slight one. She had been Cora Lane for six years. She liked being Cora Lane. She had never particularly liked being Margaret Monihan. Margaret Monihan had had brown hair and had been heavy, though sensuous. Cora Lane was brilliantly blond, slimmer, perfumed, expensively stockinged and shod, dramatically dressed.

When she had finished talking to her mother she took her shoes off and lay down on the bed to read the papers. First she read Parson's column and was pleased to find a reference to herself. "Cora Lane's dates with handsome Bill Keith," Louella had written, "are lifting a few eyebrows, but the smart money in the Lane sweepstakes is still on Mike Gordon. One report has it that they'll marry in April."

She had not been in the house for more than ten minutes when her mother mentioned the item.

"You still going with that Jewish fella?" was the way she put it.

"Mother," Cora said, exasperated.

"What's the matter?" her mother said, blank-faced.

"His name is Mike Gordon."

"Did I say anything wrong?"

"Oh, never mind."

"Oh, you mean my calling him a Jew? Well, he is,

ain't he? I mean is there any crime in mentioning that fact?"

"Not at all," Cora said. "Forget it."

She walked to the dining-room window and looked out at the old neighborhood. A feathery rain had started to fall as she had pulled up to the house in a Yellow cab, a bandanna over her blond hair, wearing a plain wool coat and her oldest shoes. The street outside, washed now in smoky rain, depressed her. It seemed smaller in an over-all way as compared to her early memories of it. The windows in the apartments across the street seemed tiny, dingy. When she turned away from the window she nevertheless felt truly at home. Her mother was in the kitchen, shelling peas, and a kettle was boiling on the stove.

"How long can you stay?"

"I have to go back to the Coast day after tomorrow," Cora said.

"I didn't mean to cause any trouble just now," her mother said, "I mean when I talked about that Gordon fella. But I was just wondering if what they say in the papers is true, that you and him is gonna get married."

"I don't know, Mom. We might."

"Is he a religious Jew?"

"What do you mean?"

"I mean how are you gonna get married? In the church?"

"I don't know, Mom. I suppose so. Anyway, it's not about to happen, so let's just forget about it."

"All right," her mother said. "I just want you to be happy, you know that. I mean Pauline is happily married and sure, poor Joe is only a good-natured, hard-working slob, but they've got two fine kids and they're getting along just swell. I want you to do as well."

Cora stared at the steam forming on the cold glass of the kitchen window. It was both good and bad, being Margaret Monihan again.

"I'm doing fine," she said. "I've got three mink coats, a house of my own in Bel Air, and the studio is giving me a big raise starting next month. Who the hell would help out around here if I was like Pauline, married to a bartender?"

"I keep telling you not to send me a penny," her mother said.

"I know," Cora said, "and it's pretty asinine, isn't it? You know you can use everything I send you."

"Well, just as long as you don't leave yourself short," her mother said.

"I don't. What time are Pauline and Joe coming?"

"About six, I guess. They won't stay long after dinner. Couldn't get a baby-sitter, I guess."

"How's Pauline feeling?"

"Oh, fine. Her back bothers her a little like it used to, but nothing serious. Oh, did I tell you Matty O'Brian died?"

"No," Cora said. However rarely she visited home, always there were the reports of deaths of old people Cora could scarcely remember. Her mother still read the death notices everyday. She seemed slightly disappointed if she did not recognize the names of any of the deceased.

At six o'clock Pauline and Joe and their daughters burst in, all laughter and loud talk and firm handshakes and kisses and awkward jokes. There were the first few uneasy minutes as always, the family wondering if she had changed too much to be one of them any more, Cora wondering if they had forgotten how she really was.

"Well, how is it out there in the land of the silver screen?" Joe cried, smiling stiffly.

"Oh, just the same, I guess," Cora said.

"We saw you in *The Sailor and the Blonde*," Joe said. "Pretty hot stuff!" She felt embarrassed at his wink.

Uncle Tom came in shortly after six-thirty, looking tired and much older than Cora had remembered him, his dark gray cardigan sweater grimy and frayed at the cuffs. A stubble of white whiskers lay upon his lined cheeks and his blue eyes looked weak and wet. When he kissed her he smelled of tobacco and beer.

"Why didn't you let me know where you were?" he demanded. "I'd have gone down and picked you up. No sense wasting good money on taxi cabs when I can drive you around. Listen," he said, "I'm off tomorrow. You want me to drive you any place?"

"No, thanks, Tom," Cora said. Through the living-room window she could see his car, an old Plymouth, parked outside, its paint devoid of sheen, one window cracked.

For dinner they had corned beef and cabbage, boiled potatoes, cauliflower, sliced tomatoes, pumpkin pie, and coffee. The sills of the windows in the dining room were dusty and the wallpaper was spoiled, but the table service was spotless.

"I'll bet you don't get good food like this out there in Hollywood," Uncle Tom said, smacking his lips. "All they give you out there is orange juice and fish and things like that. At least that's all I got out there in 1932."

"Times have changed," Cora's mother said.

"I know," Tom said, "but home cooking is home cooking. You want some more corned beef, Marge?"

"No, thanks."

"Pauline?"

"Don't mind if I do," Pauline said.

"I could go for a little more myself," Joe said.

The youngest child spilled half a glass of milk and Pauline leaped to the kitchen for a rag.

"Here," her mother said, "have more cabbage." Before Cora could protest, a second helping of cabbage was dumped onto her plate.

"Have more corned beef," Tom said.

"She said no, Tom," Cora's mother explained.

"Well, give her more anyway. She looks skinny to me." As he laughed the look of his imperfect false teeth made Cora want to pat his arm.

After dinner they all sat in the living room on the Sears Roebuck furniture and tried to keep the conversation going. It was difficult. At last Cora began asking about old friends.

"Whatever happened to Sally Whatsername?" she said.

"The tall one?" Pauline said.

"Yes."

"Oh, my God, she married a Dago and they live in Seattle now, I think."

"And Tom Conlon?"

"The one you were sweet on?" her mother said.

"Don't be silly," Cora said. It was strange, she thought. One week ago at this very moment of the night she had been lying in Ty Curtis' bed, crying and trying to get drunk because after he had made love to her he had said, "My dear, you've got quite a problem there."

"What are you talking about?" she had said.

"You know what I'm talking about," he said. "Unless you're more naïve than I thought. Tell me, frankly, do you really enjoy sex at all?"

She had tried to slap his face, unsuccessfully. And now here she was sitting with her family, feeling schoolgirl embarrassment because she had asked about a long-ago, almost forgotten love and her mother had spoken to her in a teasing tone.

"He got married to a girl from Peoria," Pauline said, moving the conversation along gracefully. "He lives on the North Side now and they have five kids, I think."

"Whatever happened to Gloria Scanlon?"

"What didn't?" Joe laughed.

"Oh, she was all right," Pauline said. "She was a little wild and all, but she finally settled down after the war, after her first husband was killed."

"She did?"

"Yeah. She lives over around Halsted somewhere," Pauline said. "She got married again, to one of big Jack Dugan's boys. They live over around Halsted somewhere."

"No," said Tom; "they used to, but I think they moved. Over farther east. And they're mighty damn sorry, I'll tell ya. The whole neighborhood is overrun with niggers."

Cora looked at the children, playing on the floor; she expected someone to chide Tom, but the conversation flowed on. What from her viewpoint had appeared to be a sudden jagged rock in the stream was invisible to the rest of them. The talk surged past the word "nigger" as it had past "Dago."

"When *you* gonna get married out there?" Tom said suddenly.

"Why, I don't know," Cora said. "There are so many fellows it's pretty hard to make up your mind out there, you know." Defensively she had been driven to make a joke of her answer.

"Let's see," Tom said, bumbling on, innocently. "Pauline, how old are you now?"

"Thirty," Pauline said. They all knew that Cora was one year older. Only her public believed she was twenty-five.

"Listen," her mother said. "Anybody want to watch the television?"

"Ah, there's nothing on any more," Tom said, "except a lot of goddamned cowboys."

Pauline's oldest daughter, aged five, said, "What's a goddamned cowboy?" and they all laughed.

Cora sat for a while, listening to the rest of them talk, looking at Joe and wondering how it was with Pauline when he made love to her. Two children. Could you become pregnant without achieving—oh, of course. She whispered the word "stupid" to herself. She thought of Ty Curtis and worked over her old anger. Mr. Sophisticated. Big talker. Call a spade a spade. Quite a problem there, my dear girl. She had thought it might happen with him. There had been flowers. Champagne. Poetry. The deserted swimming pool with the lights underwater. Violin music on the invisible hi-fi. Her schoolgirl visions of Ty on the screen, Marge Monihan's adolescent Chicago schoolgirl crush on Ty Curtis. It had all added up to something— but not quite to what she had wanted. And of course with Mike it never had come close. He was patient. Understanding. Loving. Helpful. Cooperative. Self-sacrificing. She had said to him, aching to increase her passion,

"How can you wait so long?" and he had given her his big, good-natured smile and held her very close. And none of it had done any good. During the long months Mike had gradually become thoroughly abandoned physically, experimental, almost embarrassingly so. It had not helped. As for "Handsome Bill Keith," that was a true laugh. Dates arranged by the studio. The Sailor and the Blonde. And the Sailor in actual life reserving his affections for real sailors or busboys or anything except women.

The studio pawings had not helped. The furtive attempted kisses at line rehearsals. The insinuations from married actors, agents, producers, writers. The blunt propositions. Why could she not handle it like the other women? The ones who got married, the ones who were able to laugh it off, the ones who loved every minute of it, the ones who pretended to enjoy it. She had tried that once but been caught at it. Humiliating. She smiled now, remembering that she had never really had much ability as an actress, in bed or before the camera. Pauline's children looked fat and shiny on the floor.

"Those are gorgeous shoes," Pauline said.

"Thanks," Cora said. "Not too expensive, really. I'll send you a pair if you'd like."

"Where in the name of God would I wear them?" Pauline laughed.

"Why, what do you mean, Paul?" Joe said. "We could go dancing."

"Not in those shoes," Pauline said. "I'd fall down."

Pauline and Joe and the children left shortly after eight o'clock. The house seemed remarkably quiet after they had gone. Cora, her mother, and Tom sat in the kitchen, drinking tea.

On the radiator Cora noticed a stack of movie magazines.
She picked up a handful and put them on the table. Her
face smiled back at her from two of the covers. She selected
a copy of *Photoplay* and turned to the story about herself.
There was a picture of her getting off an airplane in
Rome, a picture of her skiing with Ty Curtis (faked in a
studio), a color picture of her on the lawn of the house in
Bel Air, another color picture of her in a tight green
knitted bathing suit, lolling by her pool.

"It's a pity your poor father isn't here to see you now,
Marge," Tom said, sniffling.

The kettle sighed, seeming far away. A dog barked in
the distance. From the next block the sound of a streetcar
clattering through the night came through the substance
of the walls.

"My God," Tom went on softly, speaking as if to
himself, "imagine Billy Monihan's daughter a movie star.
What a good laugh he'd get out of that. He had a wonderful sense of humor, ya know."

"I remember," Cora said.

"Tom," her mother said, "do you remember the night
when the man in the next building came home drunk and
got into our place by mistake and put his groceries down
on our dining-room table?"

The two of them laughed heartily, stirring their tea.

Cora looked at the next magazine. The story about her
was titled "Cora Lane, Favorite Sweetheart of the GI's."
A wartime story. Cheesecake. There it was: the big picture, the shot of her standing long-legged on tiptoe, in
what looked like a man's pajama top. That picture had
been largely responsible for her success. A pinup favorite
with millions of service men. A psychiatrist at a party in

Hollywood once had gotten a bit drunk and said, "My dear lady, have you any idea of your importance as a sex symbol to our troops? Have you any idea of the number of men who have looked at your picture before turning out the lights and then assaulted you in their dreams?" Someone at the party had interrupted the conversation at that point, to Cora's complete relief; but often during the years since that night she had thought of herself in just that way, as a sex symbol, as an object desired by millions of men. She had had a dream one night that millions of men, one after the other, had made love to her and that once or twice a face had loomed up for a moment that seemed to belong to someone who had brought her almost to the point of complete satisfaction, but . . .

"Is this Gordon fella a nice guy?" Tom was asking.

"Oh, yeah," Cora said. "Very nice. Kind of like that guy I used to go out with for a while, the one from the University of Chicago, remember?"

"I remember," her mother said primly.

They fell silent.

"This is good tea," Tom said after a moment.

"Yes," her mother said.

The clock over the sink ticked noisily.

"I wonder if it's still raining," Tom said.

"I think it stopped," Cora said.

A car backfired far down the street, the distant report emphasizing the silence in the steamy room.

"Be a late spring," Tom said.

"Guess so," said Cora's mother.

Cora sighed.

"You want to stay here tonight, Marge, or do you have to go back downtown?"

"Oh," Cora said, "I guess I'll stay here."

"Fine," Tom said, "I'll clear my pipe and newspapers and things out of the back room."

Lying awake just before midnight, listening to the whisper of cars gliding by in the dark wet street, Cora felt at home and out-of-place, a child and a mature woman, a saint and a sinner. After a while she heard her mother in the toilet, heard her whisper sadly, "Oh, glory be to God," as she yawned and staggered back to her room.

Still awake at one in the morning, Cora got up, lit a cigarette, and read through more of the movie magazines, staring avidly at the more provocative pictures of herself. Her favorite, she thought, was the shot of her in the tight green bathing suit, lying in the sun by the pool, at the house where she lived in luxury and alone, the house in Bel Air.